Enslaved

Trek Mi Q'an: Book 3

Jaid Black

USA TODAY Bestselling Author

ELLORA'S CAVE
ROMANTICA PUBLISHING

An Ellora's Cave Romantica Publication

www.ellorascave.com

Enslaved

ISBN 9780972437776
ALL RIGHTS RESERVED.
Enslaved Copyright © 2001 Jaid Black
Cover art by Syneca.

This book printed in the U.S.A. by Jasmine–Jade Enterprises, LLC.

Also by Jaid Black

ℬ

Adam & Evil

After the Storm

Before the Fire

Breeding Ground

Death Row: The Trilogy

Ellora's Cavemen: Legendary Tails IV (*anthology*)

Ellora's Cavemen: Tales from the Temple IV (*anthology*)

Enchained (*anthology*)

God of Fire

Manaconda (*anthology*)

Politically Incorrect: Stalked

Sins of the Father

The Hunger

The Hunted *with J.W. McKenna*

The Obsession

The Possession

Trek Mi Q'an 1.5: Seized

Trek Mi Q'an 1: The Empress' New Clothes

Trek Mi Q'an 2: No Mercy

Trek Mi Q'an 4: No Escape

Trek Mi Q'an 5.5: Dementia

Trek Mi Q'an 5: No Fear

Trek Mi Q'an: Guide to Trek Mi Q'an

Trek Mi Q'an: Never a Slave

Tremors

Vanished

Warlord

About the Author

℘

USA Today bestselling author Jaid Black is the owner and founder of Ellora's Cave Publishing and Lady Jaided Magazine. Recognizing and legitimizing female sexuality as an entity unique from male sexuality is her passion. Jaid has been featured in every available media, from major newspapers like the Cleveland Plain Dealer, to various radio programs, to an appearance on the Montel Williams Show. Her books have received numerous distinctions, including a nomination for Nerve magazine's Henry Miller award for the best literary sex scene published in the English language.

Jaid welcomes comments from readers. You can find her website and email address on her author bio page at www.ellorascave.com.

Tell Us What You Think

We appreciate hearing reader opinions about our books. You can email us at Comments@EllorasCave.com.

ENSLAVED

ഇ

Prologue
Planet Tron, Toron Galaxy
Border-World of the Seventh Dimension
5993 Y.Y. (Yessat Years)

ഏ

"'Tis glad I am that you accompanied me on this trek to my homeland, my son."

The Empress Jana glanced up at her six-foot-three, two hundred-thirty pound boy and smiled. Squeezing his hand affectionately, she led him from the holo-port situated at the rise of the prosperous village and into a Q'ana Tal floating conveyance that drifted down towards the main trading centre below.

Four warrior guardsmen assigned to their protection led the royal procession in a conveyance directly ahead of the mother and son's vehicle, whilst four more warrior guardsmen brought up the rear in a separate conveyance behind them.

The glowing blue eyes of Kil Q'an Tal surveyed the bustling sector centre looming closer and closer on the horizon. He looked down at his mother who was seated beside him and grinned. "'Tis a passing fair place, *mani*."

Jana reached up and ran a hand over her son's plaited braids, smoothing a stray one back behind his ear. She smiled as she regarded him. "You grow more handsome by the Nuba-minute, Kil. 'Tis the image of your sire you already have."

He blushed at her words, looking away.

Jana laughed. "Mayhap such a compliment is an embarrassment to a man-child who has seen but ten Yessat Years, but in a few years more you will be happy for your good looks."

Kil grumbled at that. "Why should I have a care o'er such nonsense, *mani*? 'Tis becoming a hunter that is important."

She grinned. "Ah but when you find a special wench, the one destined to be your hearts' true mate, you shall realize that 'tis more to this life than the warring arts."

He harrumphed, doubting her words. But loving her as he did, he would not think to backtalk her.

Jana clutched his large hand in her smaller one and let the subject drop. "My *mani* and sire have not seen you in nigh unto two Yessat years. 'Tis why they asked for you to accompany me on this trek back to my homeland."

Kil smiled, warmed at the idea of seeing his grandparents once again. "Aye. The last time they traveled into Trek Mi Q'an I was gone off to Joo with papa."

Jana nodded, then released his hand to point out various familiar places she saw hovering below them. Kil listened intently, his gaze scanning the trading stalls and homes dotted about the picturesque landscape of the blue-tinted world they had landed on.

"And there," the Empress said excitedly, "is my birth home." Her sigh was wistful. "Your aunts and uncles and I spent the most carefree of youths in this village." Her lips widened into a nostalgic smile as she brushed a long golden lock over her shoulder.

As he studied his mother's face, Kil thought to himself that never had he seen a more beautiful visage. He wasn't certain if she appeared that way to the rest of the galaxies or only to him, but it mattered not. She was perfection. She was his mother. "Do you miss it here, *mani*?"

Jana's eyes widened in surprise. "By the sands, nay." She shook her golden head and smiled. "I carry many a fond memory of my childhood, my love, yet am I more content than ever I thought possible at your sire's side." She took his hand in hers and squeezed. "If I had never left Tron," she said gently, "then never would I have had you."

"Would that have been bad?" he asked seriously, his large body a mask for the simplistic and needy ten-year-old child dwelling inside of it.

Her eyes softened. "'Twould have been a fate far worse than death, my son." She placed her other hand atop his as she studied his face. "I love you, Kil."

Satisfied, he grunted arrogantly. He turned his head and watched the activity below them, too embarrassed by love words to return his mother's exclamation of caring.

Jana stifled a smile, opting to bite her lip instead. She knew her second-born son loved her. Mayhap even more than her other children did, which was saying a lot. But Kil, he had always been the neediest. He had always demanded great shows of her affection where the other three boys were content with the occasional kiss to the cheek and loving embraces.

Not Kil. He needed constant gestures to reassure him of what lay in her hearts. And just as importantly, he needed to hear the love words, even if he was too embarrassed to return them. 'Twas what made their relationship so strong and so special, she supposed.

Fifteen Nuba-minutes later, Jana and Kil strolled hand-in-hand through the bustling trading centre, stopping occasionally to purchase a trinket or two. Kil released his mother's hand when they arrived at a holo-game booth and eagerly sorted through the offerings until his gaze found the one he most coveted. "May I purchase this one, *mani*?" he asked, glancing over toward where she stood a few feet away at the next booth spraying her neck and cleavage with a sweet-smelling scent.

"Aye." She looked up briefly and winked conspiratorially before returning her attention to the perfumes. "You may have whatever your hearts desire on this trek."

He grinned, deciding on the spot that traveling with his mother was far more enjoyable than traveling with his sire.

Kil was about to turn back around to make his purchase when an odd intuition passed over him. His stomach muscles clenched inexplicably as his gaze meandered toward a warrior guardsman standing behind his mother. The warrior's fully-grown height, he noted, surpassed his own by more than a foot.

Kil frowned. He had not a care for the way the warrior guardsman was regarding his mother. The warrior's eyes continually flicked over the empress' backside, insolently sizing her up as though he had the right of it.

Jana picked up one scent after the other and sniffed them, unaware that she was being ogled from behind. Her gaze settled on a bejeweled flask of perfume a shelf down and, bending over to retrieve it, her *qi'ka* molded to her buttocks, leaving nothing of what lay between her legs to the imagination.

Kil's eyes narrowed menacingly as the warrior in question stepped towards his mother and pressed his erection against her buttocks.

Jana gasped as she stood upright and immediately whirled around to face him. "How dare you!" she spat. Her eyes widened fractionally as she studied the warrior's face. She gulped. "Who are you?" she asked in a shaky, nervous tone.

The warrior's lips parted into a mocking grin. He bowed irreverently then stood up and, his expression changing to serious, ran a large hand over her breast and squeezed the nipple. "The last fuck you'll ever have, Excellent One."

Kil's nostrils flared as his mother began to back away from the warrior. His entire body shaking in rage, he released the holo-game he'd been holding and made to go and retrieve Jana from the vile man.

A telekinetic punch in the mouth made Kil reel back. Holding his jaw, he gasped as crimson red blood trickled from a large cut on his lip.

His anger building, Kil growled as he lunged toward the warrior, knowing 'twas he who had struck him. But then, as if he had been plucked out of mid-air, two sets of hammy hands slammed down on him, throwing him to the ground and holding him pinned to it.

"Let her go!" he bellowed, his eyes darting up toward his mother.

Jana cried out as the first pretender warrior struck her, blood spurting from her nose as it broke. "Please," she begged, as her *qi'ka* was then ripped from her body, "do not do this before my son!"

Kil struggled against the hold the other men had on him, tears of horror and frustration gathering in his eyes as he watched his mother get thrown to the ground. The man who had struck her chuckled at her fright, then raised his foot and kicked her in the ribs, causing three of them to break upon contact.

Villagers began to scream, running from the trading stalls within the city's centre. The pretender warriors laughed at their fright, knowing as they did that the entire sector was now under insurrectionist control.

"Nay!" Jana sobbed as their leader mounted her broken body from behind. "Nay," she whimpered, "please—do not."

"Aye," the insurrectionist leader panted out in between thrusts, "your begging is sweet music to my ears." He grabbed her by the hair and shoved her face into the dirt, momentarily suffocating her as he raped her.

"*Mani!*" Kil cried out. "Nay—*mani!*"

Kil wrenched his body from under the hold of the other insurrectionists, his anguish giving him a strength which under normal circumstances he wouldn't have been old enough to possess at ten Yessat years. When he was free, he ran toward her at top speed and, with every bit of power he could wield and then some, he kicked his booted foot directly into the mouth of the man raping his mother.

13

The man bellowed in pain as he clutched his jaw, but 'twas not enough. Before Kil could do aught else, two sets of hands seized him and hurled him to the ground with enough brute force to crack one of his ribs.

"If you know what 'tis best," one of the warriors chuckled as he kicked Kil in the side, "you will hush your tongue that our leader will grant you a quick death."

Panting from the intense pain, Kil found the strength to narrow his eyes and spit at him, blood and mingled saliva hitting the insurrectionist square in the eye.

The man growled as he swiped the spittle from his face. His jaw clenching, he raised his foot, preparing to finish the young king off with the serrated blade that pointed out from the toe of one of his boots.

Kil turned his head at the last possible second and, with sheer luck, sideswiped a fatal stabbing that like as naught would have killed him. The twisted piece of sharp metal found his cheek instead, slicing open the side of it like a piece of meat on a platter.

"Goddess help me."

The voice was weak, broken, the words more piercing to Kil's hearts than the serrated blade had been to his face. "*Mani*," he said quietly as tears tracked down his cheeks. Restrained by the insurrectionists, he could only turn his head to look at her, watching in cold horror as the leader stepped away from his mother and granted followers who had just joined him turns at raping her.

Jana's entire body was fiercely battered, her face hideously distorted by a broken nose and jaw. Her breathing was shallow, coming slower and slower. The force of the blows she'd been dealt must have caused something to rupture inside of her for she was fading quickly.

Kil closed his eyes briefly, realizing for the first time that she was going to die. His mother who meant everything to him—she laid there dying whilst vile men thrust in and out of her body for sport.

"Nay, *mani*," he softly cried whilst the tears continued to track down his cheeks unchecked, "do not leave me."

Jana's eyes strayed slowly toward Kil's. They were so dim he knew that the light in them would extinguish at any moment. Her breaths came slower and her face muscles relaxed as the overwhelming pain numbed her until she felt no more.

Slowly, ever so slowly, as if the movement was so exhausting it took her last reserve of strength, his mother's lips curved softly to speak to him. Though he'd heard not a sound, he had known what she had said.

I love you...Kil.

"*Mani*," he whimpered. He opened his mouth to give the love words back to her, the words she had told him so often, the words he had always been too embarrassed to return. But, perversely, 'twas too late.

The lights in her glowing eyes dulled and dimmed, and the Empress Jana passed through the Rah and on into the next realm. The warriors continued to spill seed inside of her, oblivious of her death in their sickening frenzy to copulate within her.

Kil closed his eyes and sobbed as his body shook in anguish. She was dead. His beloved mother was dead.

And he'd never told her that he loved her.

Chapter One
Washington, District of Columbia
United States of America, First Dimension Earth
July 4, 1967 A.D. (Anno Domini)

∞

Having removed the poncho top she wore, twenty-one-year-old Martha "Marty" Mathews turned proudly on the erected stage to face the sea of paparazzi. She was clad only in jeans, a brassiere, a pair of Birkenstock sandals, a wreath of sunflowers about her head, and a lot of indignant attitude.

Her bravery faltered a bit when she noticed that the photographers gathered around the podium that stood near the gate leading to the White House were snapping pictures of her more quickly than she could blink. Could she really do this? she asked herself a bit warily. Could she really see this Independence Day protest through the way she and Jeannie had planned for it to go?

No justice! No peace!

No justice! No peace!

No justice! No peace!

Marty's nostrils flared in remembered anger as the fellow women's rights protestors began to chant. She mentally ticked off a list of the reasons that had brought her from Ohio to march on the Capitol to begin with.

Equal Rights.

Viet Nam.

Women in positions of power.

Freedom of expression.

The right to choose.

No more pantyhose at work—arrg!—the damn things always ran.

Growling low in her throat, Marty fervently told herself as her fingers lifted to unclasp the bra she wore that she would definitely see this protest through to its fruition. The sunflower Jeannie had painted onto her cheek twisted portently as she ripped off her bra and, with an ear-piercing roar that would put Tarzan to shame, tossed it onto the lit bonfire.

The thousands of women's rights supporters swarming below began to cheer, giving Marty the gumption to raise two angry fists before the reporters and scream like a banshee. A banshee with naked breasts. "No justice! No peace! No justice! No peace!"

The crowd began to cheer, the ruckus soon turning into a loud chant. Filled with triumph, Marty cocked her head to signal to Jeannie, letting her friend know that it was time to join her center stage and burn her bra for the assembled throng.

Jeannie's eyes widened nervously. She gulped as she glanced down into the sea of faces below. She made no move to join Marty out on the platform, opting instead to slink away unseen and scurry down the back of the podium steps.

—Arrg!

Marty's nostrils flared as she watched her friend run from the demonstration as if the hounds of hell were nipping at her heels. This entire bra-burning scenario had been Jeannie's idea, she thought grimly. And yet when push came to shove, Jeannie had left her to do the deed alone.

Turning back to face the crowd, it dawned on Marty for the first time that she was the only person in the entire assembly who was both female and topless. Nobody else had said that they planned to burn their bras with them today. She had just assumed that by the time she and Jeannie had both burned theirs, the others would get worked up into a frenzy and do the same.

17

Marty's eyes narrowed as she scanned the crowd chanting below her. Plenty of them were worked up alright, but not even one of them had removed their shirts.

— Arrg!

* * * * *

Marty cursed under her breath as she walked briskly through the camp that had been set up by the protestors as a communal housing facility during their stay in the nation's capitol. The commune lay just twenty minutes outside of Washington D.C. in a forested area of Virginia.

Determined to ferret Jeannie out and kill her, she was frustrated and more than a little disappointed when a male protestor who went by the nickname Peaceman informed her that Jeannie had already packed up and went back home.

"I don't believe it!" Marty snapped, her hands flying up to find purchase on her hips. "She went back to Toledo?"

"Jeannie's jig was up," Peaceman declared in low tones, his eyes flicking suspiciously back and forth to make certain no police were looming in the vicinity. "The fuzz must of threatened to take her in to get her to leave." His lips tightened. "I hate the damn cops!"

Marty sighed, realizing that Peaceman was as high as a kite. She doubted she'd get much useful information out of him. And she also doubted that Jeannie had fled Washington to elude the police. No, she thought with down-turned lips, she had probably fled to elude Marty's wrath. Jeannie, she conceded grimly, was smarter than she looked.

"You know, Marty," Peaceman slurred, his green eyes scanning over the poncho top and bellbottoms she wore, "that was one bitchin' show you put on today."

Marty nodded, warming to the topic. She had worked long and hard to make certain everything would go off today without a hitch. And for the most part it had. If she overlooked the fact that she'd been chanting on a podium bare-breasted and alone.

"It came from my soul, Peaceman." Her eyes narrowed in speculative contemplation. "It was past time to show the pigs in government that the women of this country will be oppressed no more. We will subvert the dominant paradigm and reclaim our ancestral rights as foremothers to this nation and people."

Peaceman's hazy eyes clouded over impossibly more. His face scrunched up into a look that clearly said he had no idea what she was talking about. "All I meant was you've got a great set of tits." He scratched his head as he regarded her, the leather headband he wore with a peace sign carved into the middle of it crinkling along with his forehead. "But the rest of what you said sounds pretty groovy too."

Marty's lips pinched together in a frown. She harrumphed as she walked away, deciding that some comments didn't deserve a reply. Especially when the one doing the commenting had smoked so much marijuana she doubted he'd remember their conversation an hour from now.

Well, she thought with a sniff, at least something had come of this day. A man had told her she had a great set of tits.

— Arrg! What a damn day!

* * * * *

For the next forty-five minutes, Marty ambled about the forested commune grounds aimlessly, her only objective to take a brisk walk — alone. Campfires were lit up all over the place, the smell of burning incense and marijuana so overwhelming that her eyes began to water.

She could hear guitars being strummed around campfires in every direction, the other hippies who'd sojourned to the capitol mellowing out after today's Independence Day protest and in preparation for tomorrow's trek back to their various homes.

"Peace."

Marty nodded at a fellow protestor and exchanged the peace sign with her as she continued walking through the communal grounds without stopping to chat. She was, quite simply, in no mood to be around other people.

A few minutes later, her pace slowed as she found herself next to a narrow riverbed she hadn't noticed before. But then again, she'd never ventured this far toward the commune's periphery either.

The sound of something whizzing by and landing with a dull thud jarred the ground, shaking it for a solid mile in either direction. Marty gasped, coming to a dead halt at the edge of the river.

Her eyes narrowed in confusion. She waved her hands agitatedly about to clear the air of marijuana smoke, trying her best to get a good look at whatever it was that had just landed a foot away from her.

There it was.

"A meteorite," she murmured, kneeling down beside it at the river's edge, "groovy".

The misshapen chunk of charred mass looked scalding hot to the touch, so she didn't put her hand anywhere near it. A bizarre atmosphere seemed to surround the piece of rock, warping the air all around it.

Marty shook her head to clear it, deciding she'd inhaled too much second-hand marijuana smoke. The air surrounding the meteorite was filled with static and nonsense, much the way a television looked when no programs were airing on a particular channel.

"I'm losing it," she said dully, clamping a hand to her forehead, "this is too weird."

A whizzing sound pierced the air again, causing Marty to gasp and look up. Her clear gray eyes barely had time to register the fact that a second and much larger meteorite was catapulting down from the heavens before it fell, a broken off chunk of it striking just inches from her body.

"Shiiiit!"

Marty screamed as the larger chunk of solid mass struck the river with such force that she was lifted off of her feet and hurled into the water with a strength that should have broken every bone in her body but didn't.

She broke the surface of the cold river and plummeted under, the shock of the icy temperature a sharp contrast to the humid nighttime air above. She was moving fast, so incredibly fast that—

Her eyes jolted opened and widened.

Marty realized with an acute sense of panic that not only was she underneath the river's surface, but that she was also hurling at an astounding speed straight toward the chunk of rock whose landing had thrown her here to begin with. She mentally screamed, knowing she would die when she struck it.

But no, she didn't die. She—

Oh god, what was happening!

Marty saw a flash of light and then suddenly her entire world twisted and skewed. She kept moving and moving—so fast—faster than a bullet—faster than what was possible.

Her entire body catapulted through the fuzzy atmosphere surrounding the meteorite and then surpassed it. She kept going and going and going—faster and faster, further and further.

But to where? What was happening!

She shot out of the fuzzy air and everything around her seemed surreal, as if she was floating at a warped speed in some sort of purple void. She fought with herself to keep from screaming, to keep from sucking in lungfuls of frigid water that would drown her, her entire body in fight or flight mode.

She was going too fast—she could make sense of nothing.

21

Marty continued to hold her breath lest she drown. Her eyes darted to the left of her—and did a double take. What she saw damn near frightened her enough to cause her to release her breath and scream.

She saw herself.

And then she was in front of herself, traveling at such intense speed she had left herself behind.

Left herself behind?

If Marty had known the first thing about traveling faster than the speed of light, she would have known why she'd seen and then surpassed herself. She would have known that she was hurling through the dimensions of time and space faster than the eye's retina could catch and hold onto an image.

Oh god! her mind screamed out in agony, *what is happening!*

Her face began to turn as purple as the void she traveled in when the need for air grew paramount. She was going to die, she thought hysterically. She was going to—

Her body catapulted through a fuzzy atmosphere, leaving the purple behind. She glanced upward as the static began to clear and realized she was about to break through a surface of water. She willed herself to make it, to hold her breath for just a few seconds more…

She came up gasping for air, sucking it in by the lungful. She closed her eyes briefly while she continued to tug in the air, drinking in the nourishment of oxygen as her cells stabilized and calmed. She remained that way until her lungs quit burning and she was able to breathe semi-normally.

Marty opened her eyes slowly—and whimpered.

"Where in the hell am I?" she murmured.

Her eyes wide with disbelief, Marty swam slowly towards shore, noting simultaneously that the water she was submerged in was as silver and gleaming as a mirror. When she reached the bank of the shore, she slowly climbed out and stood there as if paralyzed. Nothing was as it should be.

Four full moons hung down from the black sky, each of them a dull blue. For as far as the eye could see in what was presumably nighttime wherever it was she had been catapulted to, the majority of the ground was made of a glistening, rock-hard gemstone of some sort. The gemstone was a pearly bluish color, seemingly translucent yet opaque at the same time.

The pearly blue ground was broken up by occasional patches of florescent shrubbery, neon-like plant life which came in about three or four different hues of blue. Marty bent down to run a hand over it, snatching it back with a yelp when it bit her.

Swallowing roughly, she stood up and got as far away from the carnivorous shrubbery as was possible. She glanced down at her hand, ascertaining at once that the bite was deep and she needed help.

"Oh god," she breathed out, "where am I?"

Marty stepped onto the next thatch of pearly gemstone ground, careful to hop over the blue shrubbery positioned in between gemstone patches. A sickening wave of nausea and dizziness overwhelmed her, inducing her to clutch her heart and gasp for breaths of air.

"H-Help m-me," she panted out, stumbling aimlessly backwards. Unthinkingly she stepped into a patch of shrubbery, garnering herself a few sharp nicks on the ankle.

"Oh no. Oh g-god no."

Marty's eyes widened in horror when she realized that the plants were killing her. They had bit her and pumped poison into her—now they merely waited for her to collapse of heart failure so that when her body fell limp, they could dine on her at their leisure.

Sucking in huge gasps of air, she stumbled back towards the bank of mirror-silver water, as far away from the plants as was possible. Her lungs burning, she came down onto her hands and knees before the water and absently glanced into it.

"Oh Jesus," she whispered.

Marty's heart rate soared and her clear gray eyes widened into the shape of silver pools when she caught sight of her own reflection. She did a double take. The reflection was mirror-clear—and horrifically confusing.

Her blonde hair, once short, had grown out as if it hadn't been cut in over a decade. Her face, once chubby and rounded like that of most girls in their early twenties was now contoured and matured with sleek lines and sculpturing.

"What is happening!" she cried out, her confusion and fright multiplying in leaps and bounds.

Another wave of dizziness and nausea assailed her, causing Marty to clutch her heart and gasp. So many questions reeled through her mind as she collapsed onto her side and panted for air.

Where was she? What was happening to her? Why did she look as though she'd aged ten years? Why did she *feel* as though she'd aged ten years?

"I w-want to go h-home."

There was no home to go to, only Marty didn't yet realize that. As she fell limp onto the water bank from the poison that the plants had injected into her, she had no way of knowing that home as she knew it was no more.

In what had amounted to a mere minute of high-speed travel to Marty, ten Yessat years had passed by. Back on earth, her friends had married, bore children, their children had bore children, and then they had died.

Jeannie's body, a body that had belonged to a woman who had been a great-grandmother to a brood of seventeen, lie six feet below the surface of the earth in a steel coffin, the headmarker protruding from the soil above it proclaiming her to have died thirty years past.

Chapter Two

Palace of Mirrors, Dominant Red Moon of Morak
Trek Mi Q'an Galaxy, Seventh Dimension
6040 Y.Y. (Yessat Years)

ᔓ

Kil Q'an Tal, the King of Tryston's red moon Morak, High Lord of the Kyyto Sectors, and the newly crowned King of planet Tron, ran a large hand through his midnight-black hair and sighed. "I ask that you speak not of this to Rem." His fingers fell atop the red crystal table he was seated at and drummed out an absent beat. "'Twould do no good and mayhap a lot of bad."

Death, High Lord of the Jioti Sector, inclined his head in agreement. "'Tis true, your words."

Kil grunted as he telekinetically summoned himself a goblet of *matpow*. "In less than two Yessat months time we are slated to go questing yet again for my brother's Sacred Mate." He waved a hand about dismissively. "I shall look into the matter and deal with it before we leave for the first dimension."

"'Twas my belief you would wish it this way," Death grumbled.

"Aye." Kil took a large swallow of *matpow* before setting down his goblet. "For seventeen Yessat years Rem has actively searched the galaxies for whatever wench was born to be *nee'ka* to him. Let us pray to the goddess that he finds this nameless female before devolution finds him."

Death nodded, his expression grim. "It grows worse."

"'Tis true." Kil sighed. "And 'tis why I want him absent from anywhere that bloodshed might result."

Death raised one dark eyebrow, inducing the tattooed skull on his forehead to crinkle a tad. "Are you in need of aide on Tron?"

"Nay." He waved that away. "If 'tis true an insurrectionist party has infiltrated the planet, I am rest assured it could have happened in but one sector." At Death's furrowed brow Kil explained, "On the far side of the planet lies the blue-rock sector of Wani. 'Tis the only of the planet's six hundred sectors that has yet to be conquered and forcibly brought to heel." His grim smile was arrogant. "'Tis time to conquer...and bring to heel."

Death grunted in such a way that Kil knew the High Lord was questioning why he hadn't conquered Wani at the same time he'd brought the rest of Tron under his dominion. The answer was simple. "When my hunters first invaded Tron 'twas during one of Rem's...spells." He shrugged unapologetically. "I was more concerned with getting Rem to Ari for spiritual cleansing than with winning bedamned Tron."

"And after?"

"By then insurrectionists had invaded another Border World and my hunters and I were busy putting down the rebellion."

"Ah. So this is the first opportunity you have had to deal with the Wani."

"Aye." Kil's glowing blue gaze narrowed. "But deal with them I shall."

Death's lips curled wryly. "I never doubted you."

Just then a lushly curved bound servant adorned in a costly *qi'ka* skirt strode up to the raised red table bearing a tray of fruits and sweets. Death could surmise by her finery that she held a place of honor in the king's harem, which could only mean that she was lusty in the *vesha* hides. His manhood hardened just looking at her, her dark-haired beauty and firm breasts desirous to gaze upon.

Kil took note of Death's glazed over expression and had to stifle a grin. "Aye," he said dryly, "she's a lusty fuck. Say the word and Typpa is yours for the moon-rising."

"Aye," he grumbled, "I want her."

Typpa strolled over to Death and smiled coyly as she offered him a fire-berry from the tray she carried. The eight-foot giant leaned in closer to her chest and, forgetting about the piece of fruit, slurped a nipple into his mouth instead. One of his large hands wandered up the servant's thigh and parted her *qi'ka* skirt, his fingers running through the black curls of her mons until he found her clit to fondle it.

Typpa shuddered, her eyes closing as she leaned in closer for more stimulation.

Kil chuckled as he rose to his feet, deciding 'twas time to ready his hunters. "I grant you the use of all of my bound servants and *Kefas* whilst I am gone." He waggled his eyebrows. "Enjoy."

Chapter Three
Village of Wani, Far Sector of Planet Tron

ॐ

Marty came to slowly, her eyes blinking a few times in rapid succession as they adjusted to the bluish lighting in the room she was inhabiting. An attractive dark-haired woman who looked to be no more than twenty-five stood above her, smiling down to her from next to the bed where she lay.

Marty blinked rapidly a few times more, the blinks coming further and further apart as her eyes fully adjusted to the blue light and she got her first good look at the brunette. Her gray eyes widened as her jaw dropped open, and she stared unblinking at the seven foot tall female looming over her—a seven foot tall female with neon-pink eyes.

Shit!

Marty swallowed a bit roughly as her eyes flicked over the brunette. If she had thought that the neon blue predator plants were the most frightening specimens in existence, that call had clearly been made before she'd had a gander at the hulking woman standing before her.

The brunette was not only tall, but she was also fiercely muscled. Her body was firm and powerful, the muscles ripped into a steely perfection. Yet her curves were soft and feminine, proof positive beyond her beautiful face that she was indeed all woman.

The brunette's clothing—if one could call it that!—was odd, to say the least. It consisted of only a black leather-like bra and a black leather-like gee-string, both of which had been strategically cut into thin leather straps so that the woman's private parts were completely exposed. Other than that the woman wore nothing save a shimmering blue ring around her left nipple, a tiny blue navel ring that tinkled ever so slightly when she moved, and a pair of black leather-like combat boots that ran up to her mid-thighs.

Her gray eyes narrowed. She really must have inhaled too much marijuana smoke.

"Gjykka tipa frek?"

Marty's gaze flicked about warily for the first time. Her tongue darted out to wet suddenly parched lips. Not only were the stranger's words definitely not English, but they had also been rumbled out in the deepest, manliest voice she'd ever heard.

Well, she thought grimly, the hulking brunette was definitely not an American women's rights protestor. If she was, she decided on a sudden pang of female camaraderie, the demonstrators would have won the Battle of the Sexes using only Attila the Huntress here as their weapon. One look at her and the opposition would have went running for the hills. "Um...huh?"

The gigantic woman cocked her head to study Marty. She repeated her question loudly enough — and manly enough — to wake the dead. "Gjykka tipa frek?"

Marty flinched. Uncertain what to do or say, she slowly shrugged her shoulders to indicate as much as she met the brunette's neon — pink! — gaze.

Neon pink? *Arrg!*

"I don't know what you're saying," she said slowly and distinctly. Her gaze flicked down and she noticed for the first time that her golden-honey hair had indeed grown down to her butt. She hadn't been dreaming up that bit after all.

Wearily, Marty clapped a hand to her forehead and sighed. Whatever was happening to her was weirdness incarnate. Her honey-gold hair had grown down to her butt, she'd aged ten years outside of a minute, she'd been attacked my killer neon-blue plants, only to wake up and find that she'd been rescued by a nearly naked seven foot tall woman with neon-pink eyes who could beat any man Marty had ever seen to a bloody pulp with one swoop.

This, she decided, was definitely not groovy.

—Arrg!

The brunette's brow furrowed as she regarded Marty. The gigantic woman slowly nodded her comprehension as it apparently dawned on her that the wee woman she'd rescued couldn't understand a word that was being asked of her.

The Amazonian-esque brunette held up a finger, indicating she would be back. Marty inclined her head in understanding, then watched as the woman's leather gee-string clad buttocks wore a path from the room.

The door slid closed behind her with a whizzing sound, locking.

Marty gulped.

Marty's eyes flicked nervously about the room as she threw aside the exquisitely soft animal pelt that covered her, preparing to find a way out of her predicament. She had no idea why the woman had locked her inside, but she mentally supposed that such an action didn't bode well.

She had gotten no further in her escape attempt than alighting to her feet when it occurred to her that she was completely naked. "Damn," she muttered under her breath as her hands instinctively raised up to shield her breasts, "now what do I do?"

Marty was given no time to answer her own question for the door slid open a moment later, revealing the brunette who had saved her from the killer plants as well as two more hulking female giants garbed in the same black leather at her side. All three women were possessed of neon-pink eyes.

Marty bit down on her lip and began to slowly back up.

The brunette held up a palm as if sensing Marty's fear. Her voice was deep but soft, as if trying to coax her into calming down. "Gyat mekka ph'im." *We mean you no harm.*

Marty felt tears gathering in her eyes, partly from frustration because she had no idea what was being said to her, and partly from fright. She'd never seen women so huge. She'd never seen men so huge. And she'd certainly never seen anyone with neon-pink eyes.

She had no clue as to what was going on, but she knew that something beyond her understanding had happened. These women were real—very real—and they were definitely not in costume. Besides, she hesitantly conceded, nobody could make their eyes change to a glowing pink. Such was not possible on earth in 1967.

"Gyat mekka ph'im."

The brunette's eyes softened as she repeated her foreign words. She looked away from Marty and glanced toward the equally gigantic females accompanying her—women who toppled Marty's five foot six stature by a foot and a half apiece—and motioned for one of them to come forward.

Another brunette strode forward from the group of three, a black leather outfit and blue shimmering rings in her hand.

Marty's eyes narrowed in confusion—then widened in comprehension. Her lips pinched together in a frown. "Forget it." Her hand slashed definitively through the air. "I'm not wearing that outfit. And," she ground out, "nobody is piercing my nipple and navel."

The three giant women looked toward each other, then back to Marty. The brunette wielding the black leather and blue rings inched forward slowly, like a snake stalking and attempting to mesmerize its prey.

Marty's nostrils flared indignantly. This was just too much. "No!"

The brunette inched closer.

"I said no!"

The brunette drew frighteningly closer, inducing Marty to have to crane her neck to look up at her. "I. Said. No." Each word was bit out through set teeth. She couldn't believe she

31

had the nerve to tell these women no to anything, but there it was. Her look was haughty as she swept a hand about. "Begin as you mean to go — *ooooon*."

Marty screeched as a pair of large female hands seized her by the shoulders and plucked her from the ground like a doll.

The brunette grinned, her eyebrows wiggling insolently as if she was daring her wee captive to do anything about it.

Marty's nostrils flared, knowing as she did that she'd been bested. Her hands balled into fists at her sides as she growled out the only word that came to mind.

" — Arrg!"

*   *   *   *   *

It had only been three weeks since Flora, Gardinia, and Tulip had rescued her from the toxin that the plants had pumped into her, but already Marty was very fond of their companionship. She found it amusing that three such hulking warrior women had been named for what amounted to flowery plants back on earth, but she had never mentioned as much to her large friends.

Besides, she conceded grimly, Tulip was extremely sensitive and given to bursts of temper. There was no point in needlessly angering a woman who toppled her by eighteen inches and outweighed her by a solid two hundred pounds of pure muscle.

Definitely not groovy.

Marty smiled to herself as she strolled over to where Tulip was standing, overseeing small naked men who labored with extremely sharp hoe-like objects to dig through the blue gemstone ground in order to get at whatever lurked beneath it. Well, she silently admitted, the men weren't exactly small. Back on earth they would have been considered rather large at around six feet in height and two hundred pounds apiece. But next to the women who oversaw their work, they had the appearance of weaklings.

It hadn't taken Marty long at all to figure out that she was no longer on earth. She'd read science fiction novels in her teens and she had known some of the leading theories about the possibility of life on other planets. The idea had taken her a day or two to get used to, but when faced with so many oddities she knew couldn't possibly exist back on earth she had actually given little mental resistance to accepting her fate.

For better or for worse, she now understood that she lived on the planet Tron in the matriarchal sector of Wani. She also understood that things were far different here than they had been back home. In this slice of the galaxy, for instance, it was females who ruled and males who did their bidding.

Definitely groovy.

And yet, definitely not.

When Marty had fought and protested for women's rights back home, she had done it with the ideology of equal rights for one and all in mind. She had never done it in hoping to subjugate men to women as was the custom of the Wani.

She sighed. There was no convincing Flora, Gardinia, and Tulip of anything. The only thing Marty could be thankful for was that, regardless to her comparatively small size, the female warriors of the sector treated her as one of their own merely by virtue of her gender.

The women of Wani had rescued her, fed her, clothed her — if one could call it that! — and indoctrinated her into two tongues previously foreign to her. By the mere laying on of hands and ten seconds worth of chanting, an elder brunette *mykk*, the Wani version of a shaman or priestess, had gifted Marty with the ability to understand both the language of the sector as well as the newly adopted language of Tron as a whole, which they referred to as Trystonni. The fact that the *mykk* had been able to do so to begin with had only further confirmed in her mind that she was no longer on earth.

"Greetings, Tulip." Marty's silvery eyes sparkled as she grinned up at her friend and conversed with her in Wani. "How do you fare this day?"

Tulip grunted as she smacked one of the naked men laboring with the gemstone ground on his muscled rear. "Greetings, Mari."

Mari. The word not only meant "little one" in Trystonni, but the warrior women of Wani seemed unable to phonetically pronounce the English version of the letter T, which had resulted in her being christened *Mah-ree*.

Tulip sighed. "I'm of the mind to sample of this laborer's charms, yet is there much work that needs to be accomplished before the moon-rising." Her sleekly muscled arm snaked around the laborer from behind and she began to absently stoke his penis, causing the smaller male to softly moan. The look on her face grew worried. "The *mykk* has had a vision."

The seriousness of Tulip's expression caused Marty to forget about her embarrassment of watching the warrior woman masturbate a naked man and concentrated instead on her words. "What sort of vision?"

Tulip's neon-pink eyes were troubled. "My elder sister Flora was present when the vision overtook the mystic. The *mykk* claims that trouble shall reach our sector before a fortnight passes."

"More insurrectionists?" Marty murmured. Flora had already apprised her of the three previous occasions during which rebels had tried to overthrow the women's rule in Wani. All three times the female warriors had bested them, ousting them from the village but days later. It was the stuff of legends amongst their Scribes.

"I fear not." Tulip sighed, her hand working up and down the length of the male laborer's shaft more briskly. His groans became louder, indicating that he was about to orgasm. "The *mykk* senses a threat far more powerful, but from what she cannot say."

"That doesn't sound good."

"Nay. 'Tis anything but."

The laborer spewed a moment later, his entire body shuddering as he came on a groan. That quickly Tulip forgot him and turned to give Marty her full attention.

Her glowing pink gaze surveyed Marty's entire body, from the black combat boots she wore, to the thatch of honey-gold curls between her thighs which was exposed by the black leather strips that made up the Wani version of a gee-string, to the breasts and pierced left nipple that jutted out from the cupless black leather bra donned by their people. "'Tis important that we ready as many fighters as possible. Your lessons in the warring arts shall commence after the noon repast."

Marty giggled, jumping up and down in her excitement. The shimmering blue navel ring she wore made a tinkling sound from the brisk movements. "Finally! I didn't think you'd ever get around to it."

Tulip studied her face a bit sadly. "'Tis a wee one you are, Mari, but even the smallest amongst us can bring the mightiest to heel. Never forget those words."

Marty's smile faltered a bit as she regarded her giant of a friend. She'd never seen such a sadness overcome Tulip, a woman who hardly ever expressed any emotion at all. That she appeared to be overwhelmed with grief made her words all the more disturbing.

It made Marty wonder if the shaman had envisioned more than what Tulip had admitted.

Chapter Four

ഔ

Kil's eyes flicked about distastefully as he surveyed the blue-tinted landscape of Rock City on Tron. He was so besieged with memories, and so desirous of leaving this place, that it took him a suspended moment to recall that he had asked a question of the little man standing before him.

"You were saying?"

The smaller humanoid met his king's gaze and continued on. "'Tis the women warriors of Wani who rule the sector, my king."

One black eyebrow rose up slowly. Kil found himself intrigued. He had heard rumors of a sector ruled by women warriors. He had not known until now that the rumors were true. "Do tell."

"Well," the humanoid male stammered out, his hands clamped together and twisting to and fro in a nervous fashion, "'tis not much to tell I fear. The women of the sector have ruled it for thousands of Yessat years." His next words were hesitant. "I think you will find much resistance at their hands do you try to change the way of it there. 'Tis nigh unto hideous what they do to interfering men."

Kil grunted. He had no intention of changing their day to day living, but he needn't say as much to the humanoid. 'Twas no business of the little man's. Nevertheless, he was desirous of making certain the Wani understood that whether they had a care for it or not, he was now their king. They would pay unto him allegiance and taxes. They would harbor no insurrectionists in their midst. 'Twas all he had a care for.

Leastways, Kil conceded as his glowing blue gaze assessed the weakling of a High Lord who stood before him,

36

the women warriors of Wani might prove beneficial and skilled underlings. 'Twas more than he could say for the soft men of this planet. 'Twas no wonder insurrectionists forever plagued them. A weak lot, the whole of them.

"And 'tis for a certainty that these wenches are not rebel sympathizers?"

"Aye, my king." The High Lord nodded quickly, his brow sweating. "'Tis a vow."

Kil inclined his head. 'Twas good news to hear. It meant that his work on Tron would not be overlong. He could leave this bedamned planet the soonest. All he had to do was verify the words of the High Lord as truth and he could return to Morak—and his harem.

Kil's eyes clashed with the sector leader's, inducing the little man to gulp. The scar on his right cheek twisted. "Give me the coordinates to the sector," he rumbled out. "Now."

* * * * *

"Hi—yeeee!"

Marty shouted out the expletive as she jumped to the ground from her perch atop Flora's shoulders. Armed with a *bryyit*, a silver gun-like mechanism that shot out liquid fire instead of bullets, her lips twisted in grim satisfaction as she faced down her make-believe seven foot tall holo-opponent.

She was gonna get him. Oh yeah. The pig was dead meat.

Growling low in her throat, Marty fell to the ground and rolled. Mere moments later, she shot up to her feet and aimed the *bryyit* at the holo-image. She pulled the unlocking mechanism and, in one swift move, charred the holo-opponent to a burnt crisp.

The sound of applause from her comrades in arms caused Marty to puff up with pride. Grinning from ear to ear, she turned around to face them, bowing as if she'd just finished delivering a rather stunning theatrical performance.

The warring arts, she conceded with a sniff, were pretty damn fun.

"'Tis a fine job you did, Mari." Tulip barked out the words, the pride in her voice evident. "Come. Let us make merry this moon-rising with drink and feasting. The morrow brings another day—and more lessons."

Flora grunted out her agreement. "Gardinia awaits us in yon pub. Let us be gone."

Marty nodded. Her expression was solemn as she spoke to her large friends. "Before we go, I want you both to know that I realize the debt I owe you." She smiled. "The three of you saved my life. Come what may, I will fight with you to the bitter end."

Tulip slapped Marty affectionately on the back, causing her to grimace painfully. "You wear the rings of the Wani well, Mari. 'Tis a wee warrior you are, but a warrior nevertheless."

"Thank-you," she croaked out.

From across the expanse of chipped blue gemstone ground, the *mykk* watched the trio stroll away. Her wizened eyes raked over them as they continued on to the pub, the lot of them in ignorant bliss of the events predestined to unfold.

He would come for her, she knew.

He would fight for her, she knew.

And the female warriors of Wani would fight back to protect the tiny one amongst them. They could do naught else, for 'twas their way.

But they would not win.

She sighed, turning on her heel to walk back to her cottage.

Chapter Five

∞

Kil shook his head slightly and sighed. He turned toward his captain and paternal cousin, High Lord Jek Q'an Ri, and grunted. "These wenches think to fight us."

The look upon the king's face was so surprised, Jek couldn't help but to grin. "Aye, Mighty One, 'tis also what it looks like to me."

Kil's eyes widened incredulously. "Do they not realize we can fight them telekinetically as well as physically?"

Jek stifled a smile, opting instead to make certain his *zykif* and *zorgs* were in place—for the fifth time in as many Nuba-minutes. Glancing across the blue gemstone battlefield, he fought to keep down a chuckle. "Mayhap not."

"'Tis war they want?" Kil shook his head, his mouth hanging open dumbly. He simply couldn't believe it.

"Aye, Mighty One."

Jek surveyed the opposition, noting that the warrior women of Wani had assumed a battle formation and were ready to strike. When he saw the crude, obscene gestures a wee warrior perched atop the shoulders of a large one continually threw towards their hunting party, he couldn't help it. His face split into a wide grin before he broke down and laughed.

Kil's teeth clicked shut. He grunted. "'Tis ridiculous, this."

"Aye," Jek chuckled. "If they would but let our scout draw near, we could inform them of the fact that you mean to let them carry on as they always have."

"But instead we must fight them in order to tell them that I mean no harm. 'Tis ironic for a certainty."

Jek shrugged, still smiling. "Mayhap 'twill be good sport."

Kil found his first grin. "'Twould be better sport if there were wenches amongst them we could claim as the spoils of war. But these wenches are nigh unto frightening looking." He shuddered. "Should I take one of them as a bound servant, 'twould be *her* that carries *me* to the *vesha* hides."

Jek's body was shaking he was laughing so hard. "Aye, Mighty One."

The king merely rolled his eyes.

The captain grinned. "Except, mayhap, for the wee warrior atop the over-large one's shoulders. But then again, the smallish warrior would spend her days throwing crude gestures your way. 'Twould be necessary to thrust between condemnations."

Kil's glowing blue eyes scanned the battle formation across the gemstone field until they settled upon the wee warrior in question. Inexplicably, his manhood hardened and his entire body began to tingle with awareness.

He grimaced, thinking to himself he must be too long removed from the comforts of his harem if he was getting erect at the shadowy shape of a harridan woman who continued to hurl insults his way. 'Twas a spanking that wee wench needed. Amongst other things...

Nevertheless, the warlord's attention had been snagged. That the wee warrior was cursing him out with every vile gesture and obscene word in the book, as well as ones she must have invented, didn't factor into his state of arousal. He wanted her—his body wanted her.

But what, he asked himself absently, did *dildo breath* mean?

Jek raised an eyebrow. "Your Majesty?"

Kil's eyes scanned over the wee warrior again, his acute gaze honing in and settling on the nipples that stabbed out from her lush breasts. The sight of the shimmering blue ring that pierced the left nipple only made his erection all the harder. He wanted to flick it with his tongue, then draw the nipple into his mouth and...

"Your Majesty?"

"I want her."

The statement was simple and to the point. Kil realized, however, that his voice sounded hoarse even to himself. He cleared his throat, hating what the bound servant to be already did to his control. "I want the wee one."

Jek grinned. "'Tis war then?"

Every heavy muscle in Kil's body corded and tensed. He had never felt more exhilarated before battling. Not ever. "Aye."

Jek nodded as he clicked on his *zorgs*. The leather-like armbands fit over either forearm and had the ability to detonate various deadly and debilitating weaponry. He would not kill a woman, though, no matter her size. If it came down to needing it, he would merely render the Wani unconscious.

Kil tore his gaze away from the wee wench who was even now biting down upon her tongue and insolently stabbing the middle fingers of each hand up at him. His jaw clenched as he patted himself down and made certain his weapons were ready.

'Twas a spanking she needed. 'Twas a spanking she'd get.

His head came up slowly and he locked eyes with the wee warrior perched atop the shoulders of the largest one. When his glowing blue gaze found hers and she gulped nervously, his lips curled into a grim smile.

She was as good as his.

Kil let loose his war cry at the same moment he telekinetically flicked on his *zorgs'* flight mechanism.

The look of dawning terror that stole over the wee wench's features as she watched his body take flight faster than a gulch beast was comical enough to make him grin.

But the ever-feared King of Morak and newly crowned King of Tron did not feel like grinning. He felt like fucking.

'Twas time to seize his spoil of war the soonest.

And 'twas time to find out what in the sands a dildo breath was.

* * * * *

"Come on dildo breath, show Marty whatchya got!"

Marty sat atop Flora's shoulders armed to the teeth with a *bryyit* and spewed out one curse word and taunt after the next. As they marched into a battle formation to face off against the male warriors standing in line across the blue gemstone field, a surge of adrenaline shot through her veins. She felt overcome with the need to chant.

Her nostrils flared and her cheek twisted portently as she raised two fists into the air and began shrieking like a madwoman. This felt just like any other sixties protest, she thought as the rush of blood took over. Minus the fact, of course, that she might be dead when all was said and done.

"No justice! No peace! No justice! No peace! No justice—"

The Wani joined in until all of them were shrieking at the top of their lungs. Well, Marty conceded, she was the one doing the high-pitched shrieking—the Wani just made bellowing sounds that could rival a platoon of King Kongs.

Good, she thought with grim satisfaction as she bit down on her tongue and gave the warrior she assumed to be their leader a double dose of the middle finger. The bellowing made them sound all the more formidable.

Not that they needed the added leverage. Granted, it was hard to assess how large the men were from so far away, but they were probably no bigger than the males of Wani village.

Kids' stuff.

Like a schoolyard bully, Marty continued to hurl vile insults the leader's way. The leader stood about a head taller than his men, which Marty figured might put him around six and a half feet in height.

Ha! The Wani warriors would make minced meat out of that guy. She could almost feel sorry for the poor SOB were it not for the fact that *he* was the one challenging *them*.

Smiling arrogantly, Marty's gaze clashed with that of the leader's.

Her smile faltered.

Marty swallowed a bit roughly, having never felt a man's gaze penetrate every inch of her being so deeply. This was more than a battle to him, more even than a contest. He meant to have her.

She wasn't given any time to ponder over that fact — or to consider how she knew what he wanted from her to begin with — for a moment later the leader's body soared into the air — *soared into the air?!* — and took flight.

Her mouth agape, Marty could only stare upwards in dawning horror as the black-haired, glowing blue-eyed leader drew closer and closer. She noted with much trepidation that the very man she had just called every curse word in creation was swooping down on top of her.

And that his musculature was twice as thick as a Wani warrior's.

And that he was over seven and a half feet tall.

"Shiiiit!"

As she leapt down from Flora's shoulders to avoid being scooped up into the arms of the gigantic barbarian, it occurred to Marty that she probably shouldn't have called him dildo breath.

An almost eight foot tall giant who was probably carrying four hundred and some odd pounds of pure muscle around might not take to such an insult very well.

— Arrg!

Chapter Six

ഔ

Kil scooped the shrieking wee wench up into his grasp and snaked an arm about her middle to secure her. A large hand settled on her left breast and squeezed it a bit, playing with the nipple as the *zorgs* flew them back to the other side of the gemstone field. "'Tis mine you are now," he murmured into her ear. His thumb and forefinger plucked at the nipple. "All mine."

Marty gulped, her eyes widening nervously. The feel of his hot breath on her neck sent goose bumps down her spine and induced the nipple he was toying with to harden all the more. When his other hand brushed through the honey-gold curls at the apex of her thighs, she found herself softly moaning and paradoxically hating herself for it.

"Stop it!" she snapped, her senses jarring back to reality when his fingers found her clit, "don't touch me!"

Kil smiled. A real smile. He felt exhilarated, every cell of his body tingled just touching her. He knew not whether 'twas the effect of the wench herself or the effect of the battling, but decided 'twas probably the combination of both. That for once Kil Q'an Tal was doing no battling, that he'd opted to capture his woman without even giving a moment's thought to warring, didn't factor into his mind.

His woman? he thought stiffly. Nay, not his woman. His bound servant. 'Twas a difference.

"Hush now," he said, slowing down the speed of their flying now that they were away from the battling below. "You knew the price you would pay if captured before you became my prisoner." His fingers rubbed her clit in methodic circles, causing her channel to drip for him. The black leather gee-

45

string she wore offered him no impediment, for the Wani wore their leather cut in such a way that mating could be done without having to remove their clothing. "You chose to fight, wee one, and now will you pay unto me five Yessat years worth of servitude."

Only five? For the first time in hundreds of years, such a length of time seemed far too short to his thinking.

Kil's lips puckered into a frown. Why did this bedamned wench rattle him so?

"Servitude!" Marty fumed. Her jaw clenched hotly. "Never! I will die first! Just kill me now, but do not try to enslave me or it is I who will kill you!" She decided to ignore the fact that what he was doing to her clit was a step away from making her eyes roll back into her head.

"Mmm," Kil purred into her ear in the deepest, darkest rumble she'd ever heard. "'Tis my good fortune to have captured such a passionate wench."

Marty swallowed a bit roughly, realizing as she did that her words weren't making him wary of her in the slightest. And really, what could she possibly do to such a gigantic man? And one who could fly no less! But, she thought resentfully, did he have to be so certain of the fact that she couldn't retaliate?

—Arrg!

"I want you to let me go."

Her voice sounded panicky, even to her. But she couldn't seem to calm herself. She had no idea what servitude to this barbarian would entail and had no desire to find out. Would he lock her into some dark, creepy dungeon where she was only allowed bread and water once a day for five years? Would he have her tortured in front of him for entertainment purposes?

Or, she thought anxiously, would it be far worse than that? What his fingers were currently doing to her clit gave her a fair idea of what at least one of her punishments would be.

But the most humiliating punishment of all, she conceded, would be if he not only forced her to submit to him sexually, but somehow managed to make her want it.

"Please stop," she softly hissed as her body began to respond to what he was doing to it. "Please..."

"Shhh," he murmured against her ear. "'Tis five Yessat years you owe me, *pani*." One hand continued to pluck at her nipple while the other one rubbed her clit in agonizingly slow circles. "I will take good care of you whilst you are bound to me."

Marty's eyes closed and her head fell back against his chest as a soft moan escaped her lips. She had never felt anything like this, had never felt anything so good. She imagined a man with such talent could get any number of women to do his bidding. So why did he insist upon keeping *her*? Just because she'd been caught in battle?

Marty's eyes flew open and her body tensed at the precise moment it dawned on her that she was allowing herself to become easy prey. She would not succumb to this man. She would not! She would —

"Oh god."

She breathed the words out gently as her eyes closed once more. He was picking up the pace of his rubbing, soaking her flesh until it dripped, hurling her closer and closer toward orgasm. Marty's nipples stabbed out, one of them hitting his palm, as her breathing grew heavy and labored. She was so aroused that she didn't even notice that they had landed, that he was standing on two feet as he held her body cradled and worked his dark magic on it.

"Mmm, *ty'ka*." The words were rasped out against her ear, his breath hot on her neck. "Come for me," he murmured. "Come for your master."

Marty's feminist instincts took over for a scarce second, the words he'd used setting off warning bells in her brain. Master. Come for your master.

But it was too late. His fingers continued to work at her clit, rubbing it and rubbing it until she was in agony. Her nipples grew impossibly harder, stabbing further out as if demanding his attention. Her body had a mind of its own where this giant was concerned and it wanted to come for him. *"Oh god."*

Marty gasped as the coils of pleasure in her belly burst and exploded. She groaned long and loud, the back of her head hitting his chest with such force that the knot she'd secured her hair into came loose and waves of golden-honey hair cascaded down to cover them both.

"Oh," she whispered, a look of bewilderment and awe smothering her features. That had been wonderful, the headiest thing she'd ever—

Battling ensued all around them. Weapons clashed. Hand-to-hand combat...

It occurred to Marty that her friends could even now lay dying, their blood spilling on the gemstone ground. And yet, she thought in a rush of humiliation, here she lay in the enemy's arms, climaxing for him as he'd told her to do.

Mortification stole over her as the barbarian gently placed her on her feet. This man had captured her, had flat out told her he meant to enslave her, and yet she had spread her legs as far apart for him as they would go—she had wanted him to finish her off and make her come.

Marty whirled around to face him, preparing to tell him exactly what it was that she thought of him. Her nostrils flared and her lips pinched together to form a glower most men would have cringed at as she turned on her heel and came face-to-face with his...

Waist.

Oh damn.

Swallowing roughly, her silver-gray eyes bulged out of their sockets as they looked up, up, up to find the warlord's face.

Glowing blue eyes. Midnight black hair secured at both temples with a series of three thin braids on either side of his head. A jagged scar that marred the right side of his face. Brooding lips. A ruggedly chiseled face that was harshly masculine and hauntingly beautiful at the same time.

And his body. Black leather-like pants. Black boots. A darkly bronzed body that was heavy with muscle and etched with battle scars. A shimmery medallion that hung from his neck laced with oddly colored gemstones. Massive arms that bulged like dark gold steel and were roped with puffy, masculine veins...

His waist. Her line of vision came up to his waist.

Marty's eyes narrowed and her lips pinched together in a frown. She could just bet why he wanted to enslave her! She wouldn't have to go down on her knees to perform certain duties, she thought bitterly.

His waist, she thought again. Her line of vision came up to his waist...

In that moment, every survival instinct that had been imprinted onto her genetic makeup from millions of years of evolution took over, causing Marty to do the very thing females have done since the beginning of time when being stalked by a far larger and more ferocious predator.

She ran away.

Screaming.

* * * * *

Kil wasn't certain why he didn't just end the chase here and now, why he didn't just snake an arm around her belly and bodily haul her up against him.

Mayhap 'twas because her running from him afforded him an enticing view of her lightly tanned derriere.

Mayhap 'twas because her high-pitched shrieks could cause sweet juice to go sour.

49

Mayhap 'twas because he was fascinated by the fact that the wee wench was able to run from him shrieking whilst she simultaneously held up both hands to give him double doses of the middle finger.

But nay, he begrudgingly conceded, 'twas none of those reasons. 'Twas simply because he wanted her to salvage some lost pride before he took her away from the Wani. He had a care not to injure the little warrior's feelings. Mayhap if she thought she was dodging him for a time she would feel less wounded when caught.

Kil scowled as the truth of it hit him.

Yeeck! Why should he have a care of a bound servant's feelings? Why should he even desire to rut in the channel of a woman who would bring him naught but trouble? Why, he thought angrily, did this wench beguile him so?

He knew the answers. He simply refused to deal with them.

Those expressive eyes, he reminded himself. That fetching colored hair the likes of which he'd never seen. That fleshy body that was so soft and womanly, so inviting to be lusted after and thrust into. Even the manner in which she glared at him—

She made him *feel*. She made him feel and he hated her for it. He had but to look at her and she made his hearts ache.

In that moment, the greatest fear Kil had experienced since the nightmare he'd lived through on Tron overtook him. She held a power over him he could not admit to—would not admit to.

She had bewitched him, he assured himself. Mayhap the wenches of her sector were skilled in such arts.

Even he doubted 'twas possible to bewitch a warrior by throwing obscene gestures toward his person, yet he would think on the subject no more.

She belonged to him, he reminded himself. For the next five Yessat years she was his possession, her body a mere vessel for his lust. He had captured her fairly in battle and she was his.

Yet as his arm reached out and his hand snaked around her belly, Kil couldn't quite suppress the rightness of how she felt against him. The sensation troubled him as nothing else could, induced steel talons to claw against the ice that was his hearts.

He was so troubled by his emotions, so confounded by them, that he didn't even take much notice when she squirmed out of his arms, then turned around and aimed a primitive weapon at him—he merely summoned it from her grasp without looking at her or thinking about it, the action instinctive and therefore not pondered over.

His arm snaked around her again, possessively clamping her to his side. He paid her no more heed at all, for his thoughts were in turmoil for a certainty. But nay, he assured himself, he had naught to worry o'er. The scar on his cheek twisted and his nostrils flared as he reminded himself that he needed no one, least of all a shrieking wee wench.

He walked alone. He had always walked alone.

He would just have to keep reminding himself of that fact.

Chapter Seven

Marty swallowed roughly as she glanced down at her new outfit. And she had thought that the clothing of the Wani was scandalous upon first inspection, she recalled with a frown. At least that clothing had been woman-proud, fashioned in a way that declared to one and all that Wani females were in charge and would take their pleasures where they wanted with whomever they wanted.

Indeed, the Wani didn't even mate for life. They would couple with a male with the intention of becoming pregnant when their biological needs became great and they were ovulating. But that was as far as a male's role extended. The Wani males had no rights as fathers and were never permitted to speak to their girl children as other than a servant. Marty didn't agree with the custom, but there it was.

She had been catapulted from a time and place where equality between the sexes was on the verge of bloom to a world where women reigned. A few weeks later she was captured in battle and her role had once again been reversed, but this time in the opposite direction.

She was a slave. A sex slave.

The very idea of it offended every feminist bone in her body.

The other women of the harem had called her enslavement "bound servitude" and had informed her that she would be released and free to carry on with her life after the passing of five Yessat years. Call it what you will, but to Marty it was still slavery. It might be a form of slavery that had an ending date, but slavery it still was.

She didn't know what to think, didn't know what to do. Everything felt surreal to her, as if at any moment she might wake up. Try as she might, she simply couldn't come to terms with the fact that she'd been captured in a war on an alien planet and thrown into the harem of a giant warlord on a red moon.

In a daze, Marty made no protest when she was led by escort from her private bedroom within the harem suite to the congregation chamber in the middle of the suite itself that consisted of nothing but a large room strewn with fluffy pillows and whisper-soft animal hides of every hue imaginable. This wasn't real, she thought as her eyes flicked about warily, how could any of this be real?

The sound of female moaning perfumed the air, echoing from within the harem suite proper. An accompanying male growl, the sound a man tends to make when emptying himself of seed, underscored the fact that her captor was in that room and had already busied himself doing what he apparently loved doing best.

Definitely not a dream.

The first thing Marty noticed as the topless bound servants at either side of her led her into the harem chamber, was that the King of Morak apparently had a greedy sexual appetite. Beautiful naked women lounged about everywhere, at least a hundred of them, all of them there for no other purpose than to give sexual pleasure to one man. The ten or fifteen bound servants who were able to get near the warlord in question were all over him—touching him, kissing him, stroking him—doing whatever they could to arouse and pleasure him.

He lay with his hands behind his head and his eyes closed, his mouth latched onto the large nipple of one servant, drawing from it.

Female hands were everywhere, rubbing over every inch of his flesh. The harem women kept their attention on one specific aspect of his body, apparently whatever part of him they'd been assigned to arouse, and did everything in their power to make that part of his body feel pleasured. Some servants had been assigned to nothing more than a calf muscle or bicep, but they put all of their sensuality into rubbing and kissing that calf muscle or bicep, making it tingle and feel sensuous for the master.

"They are preparing him for your channel," a bound servant whispered into Marty's ear. "You are assigned to pleasure his cock this moon-rising."

"Lucky wench," the topless servant to her other side murmured. "The master is especially lusty this eve."

"Indeed," the first one giggled as she glanced toward Marty, "he's been indulging himself of channel for the past several hours. 'Tis only just now that he feels calmed enough to sample of your charms."

Marty blinked. She was torn between the desire to run as far and as fast as her feet would carry her and the desire to understand how the man could possibly have any sperm left inside of him if he'd been screwing the entire day away.

She sighed instead. "I can't do this," she whispered to her escorts. "I don't belong here."

Oh god how she didn't belong here! From what little interaction she'd seen between the king and his bound servants, it was obvious to anybody with half a brain that she'd never fit in here. The harem women kept their eyes lowered when greeting the warlord they called master, they fondled him as he passed by, touching him wherever they could, they—

She sighed again. She could go on and on pointing out all of the sexually submissive overtures they made towards the big oaf, but what it came down to was the fact that she would never be like them—could never be like them.

And what's more, she didn't want to be like them.

Marty's hand flew up to her forehead. This was totally overwhelming. "You mentioned something about him having sex with the other servants to calm himself," she said tiredly. She hated that she even cared to know anything at all about this man, but there it was. "What did you mean by that?"

The bound servant standing to her right—a busty brunette named Ora—turned toward Marty with a grimace. "I'm not certain myself, Mari." Her look was thoughtful. "Leastways I have never seen the master worked up into such a frenzy o'er a mere coupling." She smiled. "Though mayhap 'tis a good thing for it no doubt means you will take Typpa's place as the harem's favored."

"Aye," the other bound servant whispered. "She walks around with such airs about her, Typpa does."

Marty harrumphed. She had no desire to displace this Typpa character as the harem's favored no matter how pompous the bound servant might be. She had no desire to be here period.

And yet as her eyes strayed toward a well-endowed brunette who was straddling the king's hips and sinking down onto his jutting erection, the oddest feeling of melancholia swamped her senses.

It was she—Marty—who belonged there. It was she who should be riding up and down on top of him, sinking his flesh into hers, moaning the way Typpa was moaning as she rode up and down the length of—

Huh?

—Arrg!

She didn't care!

But oh lord, as the coupling picked up its pace and Typpa climaxed over and over again on the king's shaft, the scene became harder and harder to watch.

"Master," his favored breathed out as she rotated her hips and slammed down onto him, "oh yes."

"Ride me harder," he murmured.

The warlord's large hands reached up and palmed the servant's buttocks, securing her to his body as she rode him. More servants were kissing all over him, touching him, tasting the saltiness of his skin, feeling him...

Marty felt her nostrils flare even as she reminded herself that she simply didn't care. Her heart sank and rend into two as the harem continued to arouse him, even as she fervently recollected that she hated the beast who was lying amongst the pillows.

"Mmm Typpa," the king growled, his deep voice a rumble, "ride me harder. Milk me."

The servant did as she'd been bade, her breasts jiggling with each movement she made as she enveloped him further and further into her flesh. The giant warrior sucked in his breath, his large fingers digging into the softness of her buttocks.

The sound of their coupling, of the servant's flesh enveloping the warlord's, of the king groaning out his pleasure, was enough to make Marty's teeth grit. Typpa's moans only further exacerbated the condition.

As if he sensed Marty's strong emotions and was trying to make sense of how he understood them in the first place, the king batted his eyelashes as he glanced around, a frown of incomprehension marring his brow.

At last, at long last, his glowing blue gaze found hers. They widened when they settled on her, having realized the extent of her hurt. And then they brightened as they scanned her topless form, giving her the sensation that her mere presence made him happy.

No, not happy. Happy was too weak.

Elated. He felt elated, as though he'd been waiting for her all of his—

—Arrg!

Marty shook her head to clear it, not having the first clue why all of these bizarre and confusing emotions were swamping her. Why did she feel the way that she did? And how in the hell did she know what *he* was feeling?

Her eyes narrowed venomously as Typpa convulsed once again on the warlord, her breasts jiggling up and down as she moaned and climaxed.

Marty felt tears gathering up in her eyes and had no idea why. It just felt wrong, so wrong. Typpa should not be touching him. She should not be —

Her eyes met the king's once again. She sucked in a shaky breath as feelings of hurt and betrayal overpowered her. He was cheating on her. He had betrayed her. He —

Huh?

Marty closed her eyes briefly as she fought with the warring emotions from within. She hated him, she loved him, she needed him, she disdained his presence, she wanted him, and yet she wanted him nowhere near her.

One set of emotions was primal and powerful, borne of instinct and intuition. The other set was borne of logic, of telling herself how she should be feeling instead of how she was feeling.

Overwhelmed, grief-stricken, confused, and a thousand other things, Marty glanced down at the fornicating king one more time before she turned on her heel and fled the harem chamber.

A pair of glowing blue eyes tracked her movements, following her as she fled from his presence. They dimmed when she left him, only able to shine brightly when she was near.

The possessor of those eyes was too damned stubborn to figure out why his hearts were sinking, why he needed her nearness. Feelings were something he had done away with as a man-child and as a consequence he didn't know why he was experiencing them now.

And unfortunate though it was, the one who was fleeing his presence didn't know enough about Trystonni mating to point it out to him.

Chapter Eight

ഇ

Kil's nostrils flared as he regarded the bound servant who had been the favored amongst his harem for nigh unto six Yessat months. "What mean you?" he growled. "What reason did the new bound servant give for refusing to commence her duties this time?"

Typpa was careful to keep her eyes lowered, a submissive gesture ingrained in every bound servant by the older ones when first captured and brought to their new masters. "I cannot say, Mighty One. Mari has been...difficult to get along with ever since you returned with her three moon-risings ago."

Kil grunted. He could just bet she had been difficult. 'Twas sorely apparent the wench had been sired of a gulch beast. "I want her brought to me anon," he barked. "I have waited already three moon-risings to sample of her charms." His jaw tightened. "I shan't wait a fourth."

Kil paced the length of his black crystal-mirror bedchamber as Typpa took her leave to see to his bidding. Why could he not content himself with his favored? he asked himself bitterly as he watched Typpa make her exit, her naked breasts bobbing up and down seductively. Why did he insist upon having Mari?

He knew he was behaving like a man-child. He had even gone so far as to pout last eve when Mari had not come to him as she'd been bade. He, king of the red moon Morak—pouting...

Yeeck!

Kil ran an agitated hand through his hair, grunting as he did so. 'Twas insanity, this.

On the first moon-rising he had granted Mari a reprieve when she had fled from him, realizing as he had that 'twould be a kindness if he allowed her an eve to settle into the way of things. He had hoped she would come to accept her new station as his possession for 'twas considered honorable in the advanced worlds to pay off one's debts.

Mari had battled against him with the Wani. The Wani had lost. Kil had captured her. 'Twas a simple mental deduction that the wench owed unto him the battle price he sought. And what he sought was her ministrations in the *vesha* hides.

But nay, he thought grimly, she had refused his summons on the second moon-rising as well, claiming 'twas time the women of the castle "subverted the dominant paradigm" and formed a solidarity of sorts. This solidarity, he later discovered, included trying to goad the other of his bound servants into refusing him the use of their bodies.

A tic began to work in his jaw. Had he thought Mari to be sired of a gulch beast? Nay, he conceded as his teeth clicked shut, the more he thought on the subject the more apparent it became that the wee warrior was a direct descendant of a *heeka-beast*. She mayhap returned to her nest in Koror each moon-rising after the rest of the palace lay abed.

Kil's hand balled into a fist and the veins on his arm bulged as he recalled what Mari had done on the third moon-rising when he had once again had her summoned to see to his comforts.

She had not only given him her nay, but she had sent a message of sorts back with Typpa to deliver to him. Typpa had refused to be the bearer of bad tidings, had feared that the king's anger would be taken out on her if she delivered it.

It had taken long minutes for Kil to coax Typpa into delivering Mari's message, during which he had repeatedly had to remind her that 'twas not his way to inflict harm upon a wench. Typpa had finally relented and, with much reservation, had at last relayed Mari's bedamned message unto him.

The message had been brief but to the point, Kil reflected with a frown. Typpa had squatted down a bit upon her thighs, bit down hard onto her tongue, and given him double doses of the middle finger. *That* had been wee Mari's message.

His nostrils flared.

Definitely a *heeka-beast*.

The sound of Typpa reentering the bedchamber broke Kil from his thoughts. He ran a distracted hand over his chin as he turned to face her. He could see for himself that Mari had not accompanied her. He had a feeling he would not care for the why of it. "Aye?" he asked wearily.

Typpa cleared her throat, blushing slightly. "Mighty One..."

"Aye?" He waved a hand dismissively. "Just get on with it."

She nodded, her eyes straying down toward his boots. "Mari has refused your summons again, my king."

His jaw clenched. "I see." A moment passed in silence. "And did she say why?"

"Nay. Leastways, nothing new."

He grunted. "The usual?"

"Aye."

He had a perverse need to clarify what the usual consisted of. "More nonsensical talk of paradigms and pigs in power?" The muscle in his cheek resumed its ticking. "Of subverting me and my lust?"

Typpa nodded.

He began to pace. He could feel his teeth gritting. "More middle fingers and gutter words, I presume?"

She sighed. "Aye, Mighty One."

He grunted. "More insults and accusations? More curses and threats of dire retaliation?" His jugular vein bulged. "More likening me to the fascist pigs of pre-World War II Europe—whatever in the goddess' holy name that means!" he bellowed.

Kil's tirade was about to escalate all the more when the bound servant forestalled it.

"My king..." Typpa glided over to where he stood, his pacing having momentarily halted. Reaching out, she ran her hand over his crotch and squeezed his manhood in the way she knew that he liked.

Kil groaned as he pressed his erection into her palm. It had been almost three moon-risings since his needs had been seen to. Three moon-risings of lusting o'er a wench who would not have him. Three moon-risings of wanting none other in the *vesha* hides but Mari. The moment she had fled from him he had set Typpa away from his body and taken to his rooms for privacy. And now he was in dire need of surcease.

"Let me bring you pleasure," she whispered. "'Tis all I live for."

Typpa continued to stroke his erection with one hand while she used her other to remove the skirt of her *qi'ka*. That accomplished, she bent toward him and brushed her lips across his belly. "There is no cock in the galaxies better equipped for pleasure than yours, master." She tongued his navel. "Let me be the one who sees to your needs."

Kil told himself to take her, to carry her to his raised bed and thrust into Typpa long and hard. Yet much to his disgruntlement, 'twas still the bedamned Mari whose charms he lusted o'er.

He ran his hands through his hair and grimaced. 'Twas for a certainty he was losing his mind.

"Later," he said gently.

Gently? He never said anything gently.

Yeeck!

Kil clapped a hand to his forehead and groaned. He was crazed, as crazed as the *heeka-beast* wench he lusted.

"Master?" Typpa said, worry apparent in her tone. "Have you the headache?"

"Aye," he moaned, latching onto the excuse the bound servant had unwittingly provided him with. "'Tis why I cannot couple these past moon-risings."

Her brow furrowed. "But two fortnights ago when you were wounded in battle and bleeding profusely, you commanded me to ride you whilst the priestess attended to your wound..."

Kil's jaw clenched. Were all of his bound servants becoming brazen, thinking they had the right of it to question him? By the sands, could a warrior not be possessed of the headache without ridicule!

"...mayhap if I summoned a priestess on your behalf..."

He winced. Yet another channel he'd have to turn down.

"...she could attend to your aches whilst I attend to your c—"

"Nay." He felt himself blushing for refusing a coupling, so he cleared his throat and turned away. "I-I need to be...alone." His teeth gritted. Did that sound as pathetic to the ears of others as it sounded to him? "I wish to ponder, uh, my headache."

He moaned again. By the goddess he truly was pathetic!

Typpa began to back away, eyeing him as though he'd sprouted man parts atop his head. Kil resisted the need to blush, opting instead to grunt as he threw a hand toward the bedchamber door. "Take yourself off to the crystal spinner and have a *qi'ka* of your choosing fashioned to your taste."

Her eyes lit up. Kil knew then that she'd opted to forget this episode in favor of lusting o'er material possessions.

"Aye, master," she said breathlessly before disappearing through his bedchamber door.

Kil released a deep breath, feeling as though he'd just won a small battle. "By the sands," he muttered, "I am nigh unto crazed." His jaw clenched tightly when he remembered why it was he was losing his mind in the first place.

'Twas because of *her*.

That bedamned irritating wee wench who made him feel like an unschooled man-child rather than a seasoned warrior to be reckoned with.

He was a feared man. The most feared warlord any galaxy or time dimension had ever known.

Yet 'twas necessary to do no more than gaze upon fair Mari and his hearts felt ready to swoon from his chest to his toes.

Kil's eyes flicked toward the bedchamber door. They narrowed determinedly.

Swooning hearts or no', enough was enough. The wench was about to find out her proper place. And he was the warrior who would show it to her.

Chapter Nine

ℬ

Naked, Marty stared out of the porthole that was located in her private bedchamber within the harem's quarters. This was, she thought reflectively, the strangest place she'd ended up yet since having been hurled from earth to—whatever galaxy she was now inhabiting. Trek Mi Q'an she believed she'd heard it called.

The only thing Morak shared in common with Tron was the inability of the people here to phonetically pronounce the English T in her name. So again, when she'd first told the damned giant her name, he had christened her *Mari*, insisting she was *his* little one.

Whatever.

Refusing to think about the fornicating beast who had enslaved her, she forcibly turned her thoughts to the habitat she was now living in. The red moon of Morak, she conceded, was appropriately named. During daylight hours a red sun dominated the skies, subverting a smaller yellow one behind it and casting a barely detectable reddish tint over the land. The tinting was barely noticeable on clear days, that is. On foggy days the air was shimmery and thick, almost like patches of red glitter littered the skies.

The nights were always the same though, she thought, as she gazed upwards into the nighttime atmosphere that existed just outside the large porthole. Rather than turning black as the nights did back on earth, the air stained a dark crimson red color, almost like that of blood. It was still dark enough that visibility was low such as it was back on earth, but red nevertheless.

Fascinating.

Equally fascinating was the structure of the palace she had been imprisoned in. The Palace of Mirrors, she had been told it was called. It hadn't taken her long to figure out how it had gotten that name.

The base of the castle itself was entrenched within a body of water that glimmered like a silver mirror. Several portholes were dotted all about each chamber that lied below the water line, casting back mirror-like reverberations of images from within. It was an interesting phenomenon, being able to look at a crystal-clear reflection of yourself merely by glancing toward the water that lay on the other side of the sealed portholes.

The only time it was possible to see the marine life that lurked within the silver-mirror waters themselves was when a creature would swim up to a porthole directly as if staring back at you.

Marty still got the shivers whenever she thought about the day she'd first been brought here. She had been glancing at her reflection in what she thought was a mirror when all of a sudden a large, fanged mouth had appeared around all sides of it. She had gasped and reeled back, not knowing what to think.

The head of the underwater beast had moved to the side a moment later and one crimson eye had stared back at her. She knew that the predator, which had the appearance of a red octopus with serrated fangs, had been sizing her up for a meal. It had proceeded to try three times to knock through the sealed porthole barrier, but had given up and swam away when it had realized it couldn't break through it.

An intelligent predator. Never a good thing.

Marty had gulped as she'd watched it flick a tentacle and swim away. The size of the mammoth creature's fangs and talons didn't bear dwelling upon. Needless to say they could have shredded her to bits in less time than it took a giant squid to obliterate a tuna.

So Marty had stayed away from the base of the palace, opting to remain in her bedchamber for the most part. The harem's quarters were located a level up from the waters, somewhere around the middle floor of the castle.

The palace itself was huge, consisting of thirty to forty floors. She could spend a week tooling about it and still never see everything inside of it.

The outside of the palace was formidable looking, she recalled. Marty had swallowed a bit roughly the first time she had seen it come into view. It rose up from the silver waters like a great ziggurat made of sleek black crystal, some twenty floors of architecture thrusting up from the waters and dominating the landscape.

When the red sun was setting it loomed in the horizon just behind the palace, giving the castle a sinister look. Almost as sinister as that of its master.

Kil Q'an Tal. A king. A warlord. Her captor.

Marty had done the best job she could in dodging him these past three nights, but she knew her time was running out. He would come for her. She knew he would.

Odd though it was, Marty felt as though she had somehow tuned into the warrior's emotions. It was like she'd turned on a radio and the frequency had stuck on one particular channel and refused to shut off.

He felt angry at her refusal to do his bidding—very angry. That anger had kept Marty going, feeding her own. She wanted him to stay angry, wanted him to hate her even, because it kept her defenses from crumbling.

And oh lord were they crumbling.

If the warrior's only emotion, even main emotion, had been anger then she would have been able to continue on this path, hoping to forever thwart him. She knew, after all, that he wouldn't rape her. It wasn't instinct that told her as much, not even her bizarre tap on his emotions. It was simply common sense and logical deduction. If he was the type to rape, she correctly figured that he would have already done so.

So why was she close to capitulating when she knew she could thwart him forever? she asked herself grimly.

The reason was simple. The damn man needed her.

Not wanted her. Not merely lusted after her. Not hoped to have her. She knew—*knew*—that for whatever reason the loathsome troll *needed* her.

—Arrg!

She was, Marty conceded, a royal pushover. It had always been that way. The softer side of her nature, the empathic side, had forever gotten in her way back on earth and was now proving to be her greatest impediment in remaining rigid in her stance to not succumb to the giant warlord.

She knew when he was brooding, could feel it when he became melancholy thinking about her, knowing she'd never come to him willingly. Last night her empathy had been so extreme she had paced her bedchamber for hours, debating back and forth within herself as to whether or not it would be so bad to give the big oaf what he wanted and let him find oblivion between her legs.

He needed her. He channeled his needs into something sexual, probably not wanting to deal with them, but she knew the needs were there. They were as real to her as the marine creature lurking in the silver-mirror waters below.

"Damn it!" Marty growled, feeling his melancholia coming over him again. "Why should I care!"

But she did care. And she hated herself for her weakness.

He had captured her in war, taken her from the Wani, declared her his sex slave, and thrown her into his harem. She hated him. Or, she conceded with down-turned lips, she wanted to hate him. But the wanting wasn't exactly making the reality happen. Because she didn't hate him.

Worse yet, Marty thought as she paced back and forth naked—she had refused to wear that damned *qi'ka!*—was the undeniable fact that she was fiercely attracted to the giant jerk.

She tried to tell herself that she wasn't, that she could never be attracted to the very man that had enslaved her, but it wasn't helping. She wanted him. Every time she thought about him she grew wet between her thighs and her clit pulsed. Actually pulsed.

—Arrg!

Marty grabbed two fistfuls of honey-gold hair and closed her eyes as she sank to the ground. She was going insane, she decided. This entire ordeal, from being catapulted from earth to being enslaved, was turning her into a candidate for a mental ward.

He needed her.

So what!

He needed her.

I don't care!

He needed her.

—Arrg!

Marty's shoulders slumped dejectedly as the truth hit her. She couldn't go on like this. She couldn't keep thwarting him. She was—arrg!—too damn empathetic.

He needed her.

I know, damn it!

Her breathing labored, she unfisted her hands from around her hair and smoothed back tufts from out of her line of vision. She sighed deeply as she sat with her legs beneath her, her eyes flicking open and settling on her kneecaps. "What do I do?" she murmured. "What do I—"

"Mari."

Marty froze. She knew that deep, dark voice. For the past three nights she had heard it in every dream, every fantasy, and every nightmare. And now it was calling to her softly, beckoning to her.

Slowly her head came up. Her eyes scanned the long, formidable length of the warlord until at last her gaze clashed with his.

She gulped. Her eyes widened.

If he had looked in the least bit angry, in the least bit hateful and vindictive, she could have thwarted him yet again. But no. As her eyes searched his, as she heard his breathing hitch and labor, she knew she was a goner.

In this moment in time, Kil Q'an Tal didn't look like a man to be reckoned with. He looked like a lost little boy, like a child who'd been separated from everything he knew and needed and was begging her to help him find his way back home.

The way that he looked at her, so mournful and with such intense longing...

Marty realized he was as confused as she was by their strange bond. It was that fact and no other that caused the last of her reticence to crumble.

Closing her eyes briefly, Marty succumbed to the inevitable. Without saying a word she stood up, walked to the other side of the bedchamber where her bed was located, crawled up on it, and situated herself on her backside. As she glanced toward her captor and her eyes met his, she spread her thighs wide apart, offering herself to him.

At first he did nothing, which caused her a moment's embarrassment. But when she noticed how he was looking at her, how his eyes were memorizing and coveting every nuance of her body, her confidence returned.

"I need you," he said hoarsely, his glowing blue gaze flicking back toward her face. "I don't understand the why of it, but I do."

Marty didn't have any time to respond to that assertion for he covered her a scarce second later, coming down on top of her and settling himself between her legs. He pressed the large erection bulging from his leather pants against her labia, rubbing it slowly around until she began to moan.

"I don't understand it either," she half groaned and half whimpered, reaching up to run her hands through his hair as he repositioned his large frame and began to trail kisses down her body. He began at her forehead, placed a kiss on her nose, more quick kisses at her throat...

"Oh god," Marty murmured as she closed her eyes and enjoyed the feel of his lips and tongue sucking at the base of her neck. His hands found her breasts and palmed them, his fingers plucked at the nipples while his kisses found their way down her throat, then lower still to the swell of her bosom.

He raised his head from her breasts, his breathing heavy, and locked gazes with her. "I have wanted," he said thickly, his fingers plumping up her nipples, "to suckle of these ever since I first saw you."

Desire pooled in her belly, coalescing into a pleasurous knot. Reaching up to smooth a plaited braid behind his ear, she thrust her breasts up into his palms simultaneously, causing a hissing sound to escape his throat. "Prove it," she murmured.

Kil groaned as he smothered his face into her breasts. He wasted no time in proving it to her, his tongue flicking at the blue ring around her left nipple, then slurping the nipple through the ring and drawing on it.

Marty gasped at the sensation, her back arching as her hips instinctively slammed upwards looking for surcease.

"Mmm," he growled as he sipped on the nipple, one large hand taking both of Marty's in his and securing them over her head, "Mmmm." He ground his hips into hers, his erection rubbing her clit through the leather fabric.

"Oh god," Marty moaned, her body thrashing under his to find completion. She wanted him to impale her, needed him inside of her.

Kil's mouth made heady slurping sounds as he continued to suckle from her nipple. His hips kept up their agonizingly slow rhythm, grinding his erection into her wet flesh and providing pressure against her clit.

"Please," she groaned as her hips reared up, "please."

His head came up slowly as he released the nipple, a half popping, half sucking sound resonating through the bedchamber as he did so. He grinned. "Not yet *ty'ka*," he purred in that dark rumble of his as he released her hands from above her head, "I would taste more of you before we mate." His head disappeared into her cleavage again, then slowly began to work its way downward.

Marty gulped, for a couple of reasons. First, because his rich, masculine voice was the most seductive thing she'd ever heard, and secondly because she was certain he'd called her *ty'ka*.

Ty'ka — warrior's hearts. Or, more literally, my hearts.

She was given no time to contemplate why he was calling her by such a meaningful name, a name she'd been told that a warrior only called the woman he mated with for life by, for his kisses were going lower and...

"Oh groovy," she breathed out, her hips arching up for him. She sucked in a breath as his lips found her navel, groaning when his tongue flicked the navel ring and made it shimmer.

"Oh groovy!" she screamed as his tongue flicked harder and harder at the navel ring. She hadn't realized the Wani ring could make a woman —

"How fucking groovy!"

Marty groaned like a mortally wounded animal as an intense orgasm ripped through her insides and exploded. She convulsed so harshly she could feel dew dripping down the inside of her thighs.

Kil was torn between laughter and intense longing. The look of disbelief on her face coupled with her strange ramblings were nigh unto comical. He grinned, his hearts feeling uncharacteristically light and happy. "I will make you feel more of this groovy in a moment, little one."

Marty harrumphed. "I doubt anything can make me feel *that* good."

One arrogant eyebrow shot up. "Oh do you, Mari?"

Her eyes widened when it dawned on her that he was taking her statement as a challenge. Good. Might as well make the most of a situation, she'd always said.

"Yes," she lied, deciding to toy with him a bit, "I doubt it." She unconsciously licked her lips, hoping he'd prove her wrong quickly.

Kil picked up on the telling sign, which caused him to chuckle. She made him feel so good, teasing him like real lovers would, not meekly submitting to his lust and boring him outside of a Nuba-minute as any other of his harem would have and did. No woman, free or bound, had ever made him feel so good. He was bewitched for a certainty.

"Well then," he said softly, his lips forging a path of kisses down her belly, then through the honey-gold curls covering her mons, "mayhap I will have to work for many moon-risings on perfecting this groovy."

"Maybe," she squeaked.

Marty spread her thighs as wide as they would go, then reared up her hips, trying to coax him into kissing her intimately. But he didn't. He teased her instead.

Kil's throat made sultry purring sounds as he rubbed his nose, lips, and chin through the thatch of hair at the apex of her thighs. He closed his eyes and basked in the simple sensation, turning Marty on more than she thought such a seemingly innocuous gesture could. It was as if he reveled in everything about her, even something so simple as this.

And then his large hands were clamping about her thighs and she knew he was getting ready to taste her. He opened her up as far as she could comfortably go and stared down at her flesh with glazed-over eyes.

"'Tis the most beautiful channel in the goddess' creation," he murmured.

Marty's breathing hitched, his words affecting her powerfully. "Then taste it," she whispered, her clear gray eyes seeking out his glowing blue ones.

With a groan he complied, his face diving into her flesh, smothering it with his lips and tongue. He kissed and licked at her labia, brushing all around the clit without touching it. The effect was to drive her mad with longing.

Marty's hips instinctively reared up as she used her hands to press his face closer into her pussy. "Oh Kil," she said breathlessly, "oh yes."

'Twas forbidden for a bound servant to call her master by name, yet the sound of it on her lips felt right. She would never call him master, this he knew. And odd, but he had not a care for her to do so.

"Mmm," he growled as his tongue at last zeroed in on her clit. "*Mmmmmm.*"

"Oh god."

He slurped the clit into his mouth and sipped on it, causing Marty to moan and writhe. At the same time the fingers of one of his hands came up and toyed with her navel ring, making it shimmer in the erotic way she'd discovered only minutes prior.

"Oh. My. God."

Marty wrapped one leg around his neck, using it to press his face into her flesh impossibly deeper. He groaned into her pussy, his lips and tongue sucking vigorously on her engorged clit. The pressure he was applying on her swollen flesh was hard and unrelenting. She slammed her hips upward on a moan, wordlessly begging him for completion.

Kil gave her what she wanted—what he too wanted—sucking harder and firmer while she moaned and thrashed violently beneath him.

"Oh god."

Marty's orgasm tore through her belly mercilessly, inducing heat to rush to her face and her nipples to harden into plump points. She moaned out his name as her hips rocked back and forth, her body craving more of him. "Kil—*oh yes.*"

When his face surfaced from between her legs, the look in his eyes was intense. One minute he had been wearing leather pants and—Marty blinked—now he wore nothing but a necklace of shimmering stones around his neck and seven and a half feet of steely bronzed muscle.

His breathing labored, he grabbed her by the hips and placed the tip of his erection at the opening of her vagina. Marty's eyes barely had time to widen at the enormousness of his erection when he groaned out "*Mari,*" and thrust inside of her, burying his cock to the hilt.

She screamed.

Kil's eyes widened. His body went completely still. "Mari?" he asked gently, her impossibly tight flesh making his teeth grit, "you are a virgin?"

Marty was so surprised by the question she forgot all about the pain. "No," she said honestly, the pain still there, but becoming somewhat bearable, "I've been with men back home."

He grunted. "But never with a warrior?"

"No."

His nostrils flared as if inhaling her scent. His eyes brightened, glowing an impossibly potent blue. She could feel possessiveness radiating from him like a tangible thing and the feeling made her as giddy as it did nervous.

To him, she was a virgin. In his culture, she was a virgin. What's more, a flash of intense premonition told her, he'd make certain he was the only warrior she ever offered her body to.

"Good," he murmured.

Kil thrust into her flesh with a growl, ringing a gasp out of Marty. His jaw clenched tightly as he thrust in and out of her with long, deep strokes, fighting back his need to pummel into her, to pound away into oblivion. He needed her channel to accustom to the size of him before he could mount her the way he wanted to.

Marty's eyes watered as her flesh slowly began to cooperate, the pain lessening more and more with each thoughtfully slow, soothing stroke he made. She ran her hands over his back, then lower over his buttocks, feeling the steely muscles clench beneath her palms.

"Mmm...Mari," he said thickly, "keep touching me. I need the touching, my little one."

"You feel good inside of me," she whispered, her fingers massaging his buttocks. She reveled in the feel of him, the way his buttocks clenched and contracted as he stroked in and out of her.

His teeth ground together. Perspiration formed on his brow. He wound a tress of her honey-gold hair around one of his fists, securing her to him, as he rotated his hips and continued to stretch and fill her.

Marty's head fell back on the whisper-soft bed, a bed that had been fashioned for a sex slave, for her. In that moment, her status actually served to further arouse her, making her feel deliciously submissive and desired. The feeling would surely pass when she regained her senses, she told herself, but for the moment she gave herself up to the master and to the pleasure he offered her as no other ever had, as no other ever could.

Wrapping her legs around his waist, she practically hissed as his body claimed hers with agonizingly slow strokes. "Harder," she moaned, "I need more."

"Mmm do you, lusty one?" He teased her with more slow stroking, picking up the pace just a bit, but not quite enough.

"Yes."

"And who do you want to give it to you, hm?"

His arrogance further aroused her. "You," Marty groaned, her hips bucking up for more. "I want you."

His jaw clenched. "Your pleasure is mine, little one."

Kil groaned as he sank into her, her words the only enticement he needed to mount her fully and ride her hard. He thrust into her possessively, sinking into her flesh in a way meant to brand her.

Over and over again he rode her, his eyes closing in a nearly maddening euphoria and his throat eliciting moan after moan, as he found oblivion in a way he never had before. 'Twas as if her channel had been made for him, had been fit to his body's specifications. Her channel was trying to milk him of seed far quicker than it should have, the way he'd often heard a warrior would spurt for none other than his—

"*Ty'ka*," he ground out, thrusting into her mercilessly, pounding into her sopping wet flesh with primal instinct. He wanted the pleasure to go on and on, to never end, but her body was milking his, was demanding his seed...

Marty gasped at the pleasure, her hips slapping upward to meet his rapid thrusts. She groaned as he mated her, the sound of her flesh enveloping his a wickedly carnal aphrodisiac. "*Kil*," she moaned as she felt a climax fast approaching, "*harder.*"

"Your pleasure is mine, *ty'ka*."

Kil rotated his hips and slammed home, mating her like an animal in full rut. He sank into her harder, faster, harder—

"Oh god."

"This channel is mine," he growled, his nostrils flaring primally. He held onto the hair he'd wound about his wrist

77

while he branded her, his tight balls slapping against her buttocks as he impaled her over and over again.

"Kil."

Marty bared her neck to him as her head fell back. Her climax violently ripped through her, the harshest and most pleasurous feeling she'd ever experienced. She moaned and groaned as she threw her hips back at him, greedily wanting to be pummeled while she came. *"Oh god."*

Kil's teeth gritted at the pleasure, the feel of her channel contracting and convulsing around his shaft too intense to hold back his spurting. On a groan he impaled himself—once, twice, three times more—then holding her body tightly to his, he emptied himself of seed deep inside of her on a roar of completion.

For long minutes they laid there as their breathing steadied, holding onto each other as if there was no such thing as tomorrow, as if they'd never be able to recapture the moment.

They were both confused. Neither of them understood what was happening, why they felt the way they felt towards the other.

For one of them—for Marty—the incomprehension was borne of cultural ignorance, of dwelling in a world where she didn't understand the rules.

For the other one—for Kil—the confusion was borne of stubbornness and pride, two strong emotions that had, for reasons of survival, been etched long ago from grief and an acute fear of abandonment.

Marty sighed with unnatural contentment as the gigantic warlord settled himself around her, wanting her closeness even after they'd mated. His eyes closed sleepily as his mouth latched onto one of her nipples and suckled from it. As if on instinct, one of his hands settled in between her thighs until he located her flesh, a large finger burying itself fully inside of her. She could feel all the tension leave his body after that and, scarce moments later, he fell into a deep, sated sleep.

Marty brushed a thin black braid behind his ear, and found herself smiling at the innocent picture the big oaf made while asleep. Drawing from her nipple in his slumber, his eyelashes fanned down and tickled her breast, while his finger stroked back and forth inside of her even in his sleep.

She didn't know what to make of him or the situation—a fact that was as frightening as it was confusing. But as she glanced toward the porthole and saw a streak of proud yellow sun daring to broach the brooding, prominent crimson sky, she told herself she would find a way to make everything right.

Chapter Ten

ဢ

Marty's lips puckered into a frown as she picked up a serving platter filled with sweet confections and fruits. She couldn't believe she had agreed to play serving maid to the big ogre and his equally big ogre friends without a fight, but she was sick to death of being in that damned harem chamber all of the time.

In all actuality, she wouldn't have minded this duty in the slightest — she'd waited tables back home during college after all — were it not for the fact that she had to serve the sweets and fruits to his friends topless, wearing nothing besides a nearly transparent sarong skirt.

The *qi'ka* skirt she was wearing this evening was a beautiful shimmery crimson. She'd found it lying at the foot of the bed when she had awoken this morning, Kil having already gone but the skirt left behind as an apparent gift.

Marty had thought little of it, assuming he had merely left it behind as a reminder that he expected her to obey the rules from here on out. And so she had decided to disobey him by not putting it on, defying him in the only way she had at her disposal.

She had changed her mind after Ora had entered her private bedchamber and had seen the skirt. Gasping, the busty brunette had picked it up off of the bed and turned to her with a huge grin on her face. "'Tis as I predicted," she beamed, her smile contagious. "You have bested the horrid Typpa for the master's attention."

Marty couldn't help but to smile back at her. Of all the hundreds of bound servants in the palace, Ora was the only one she felt a connection with, that inexplicable chemistry that forged two women as friends. "How do you figure that?"

Ora had then proceeded to explain the significance of the costliness of a *qi'ka* to her, even telling her how one could be sold at market if after she left her servitude she found herself in need of credits. Marty had listened intently, filing the information away for future use.

"I was the king's favored when first I arrived here nigh unto five Yessat years past." Ora shrugged. "'Tis well known throughout the galaxies that warriors tire of their favoreds the soonest, so 'tis best," she had instructed her as a friend would, "if you make the most of your status whilst 'tis still yours."

Marty's stomach had clenched at the thought, though she didn't know why. What had she expected, she'd asked herself morosely as Ora switched topics and informed her of the feast to come this evening—for a man who owned hundreds of gorgeous women to fall madly in love with her and want to be with only her?

Yes, she thought with a grimace, unfortunately that was exactly what she expected.

But why should she care if she didn't get it? Why should she—

Bah! What was the point in fooling herself. She did care. She didn't want to, but there it was.

"Are you ready?"

Ora's question snapped Marty's head to attention, bringing her back to the present. She blinked. "Yes. I'm right behind you."

Ora threw a commiserate glance her way, then smiled in a manner meant to calm her. "'Twill be all right, Mari. The feast will last but two Nuba hours at best." She sighed. "But 'tis best do I warn you..."

Marty raised an eyebrow but said nothing.

Ora sighed again. "If one of the master's honored guests desires to sample of your charms, 'tis your duty to couple with the warrior."

Marty's heart began to race. Blood rushed to her head and pounded at her ears. *"What?"*

Ora shrugged helplessly. "'Tis the way of this world, Mari." She studied her friend's face for a moment then grinned. "Truth be told, 'tis not such a bad duty at all. As you're about to find out, there is no such thing as an unattractive warrior." She chuckled at her mortified look. "Truly, if you would but look upon the situation as a dispassionate observer, you would realize that my words are true."

Marty could only gawk at her.

Ora's chuckle evolved into laughter. She wiggled her eyebrows comically and grinned. "Wait until you see the master's guests. Go on." She waved a hand toward a set of black crystal double doors that separated the kitchens from the dining hall. "Take a peek."

Drawing in a deep breath, Marty set down the serving platter onto a counter and begrudgingly complied. Ever so quietly, she opened the doors just enough to glance out, her gray eyes scanning the great hall on the other side of them.

There was Kil.

Her eyes narrowed menacingly when she noticed that Typpa was standing behind him as nearly naked as she was. The bound servant was rubbing the warlord's massive shoulders from behind while he drank his *matpow*, her breasts stabbing seductively against him.

"Typpa," she gritted out to Ora without removing her gaze from Kil and the bound servant, "is rubbing herself on him. She's even rubbing her nipples against his face and prodding him to suck on them."

— Arrg!

"Hmm," Ora murmured thoughtfully. "Then mayhap 'tis best if you do all in your power to inflame his senses."

Her nostrils flared at the challenge. "How?" she ground out.

Ora didn't think it was possible for Marty to make him jealous for warriors became jealous only when males paid attention to their Sacred Mates, so she said instead, "Let him see how desirable you are to his guests. Subtly flirt with them, make them desire to sample of your charms. If he sees that the other warriors covet you strongly, mayhap he will order you to his own bedchamber instead of to the bedchamber of one of the others."

Angry, and more than a little hurt, Marty knew she would at least give Ora's advice a try. "A warrior's way of showing off his—" Her jaw clenched. "—spoils of war?"

Ora chuckled, not at all perturbed by the notion. "Aye." She licked her lips. "But be a good friend and save the king's cousin for me." She shivered deliciously, her nipples hardening when she thought about him. "I have been desiring Lord Jek for nigh unto two Yessat years, when first I saw him."

"Which one is he?"

Ora came up behind her and glanced out the crack through the doors. "The one to the master's left," she whispered.

When Marty saw him she did a bit of shivering herself, though not for the same reason. The warrior was handsome, yes, for he looked strikingly similar to Kil. But the look upon his face was cold—stone cold. Like he'd kill anyone or anything that dared to approach him. "He's all yours," she squeaked.

Ora began pointing out the different warriors gathered around the raised table—a table that was literally suspended a few inches off of the ground as if possessed of magic—telling her which ones were the best lovers in the *vesha* hides.

"Aside from the master himself, out of all of the warriors I've tried," Ora continued in a whisper, "'tis Lord Death that gives the best impaling." She chuckled softly. "His lust is insatiable."

Marty gulped. Death was as frightening looking as Jek, perhaps more so. Jek appeared rather grim, whereas Death appeared rather...well, no word could quite describe him. When he stood up to stretch out his back muscles, her eyes widened as she realized he was at least four or five inches taller than the rest of the warriors, Kil included.

Shit.

"He is rather handsome," Marty conceded, studying his heavily muscled body and harshly masculine face. She grimaced. "But why the tattoo?"

"No one knows," Ora murmured. "There have been many rumors o'er the Yessat years, but none ever confirmed that I've heard tell of."

Marty's mind was made up. Not only because the giant was handsome, but because it was obvious that he and Kil were friends. Death was definitely the one she would be flirting with.

"Ok," she said firmly as she quietly closed the doors and turned around to face Ora, "I'm ready."

Ora nodded. "Remember to flirt."

"I will."

"You need to look, feel, and act as though you were born to seduce."

Marty bit her lip. Her confidence began to waver as she considered the fact that she'd never set out to seduce any man in her entire life. It wasn't the sort of thing that came up in the midst of a bra-burning demonstration. "How?"

Ora smiled softly, her gaze flicking over Marty's naked breasts and barely concealed mons. She pressed in closer to her friend until their nipples touched, causing Marty to blush.

"No blushing," Ora murmured, as she rubbed her nipples against Marty's, inducing both sets to plump up. She reached down and parted Marty's *qi'ka*, and ran her fingers over the honey-gold mons. Her thumb began to circle her clit, causing Marty's breathing to hitch.

"When you feel turned on," Ora whispered, "you feel as though you were born to seduce." Her thumb continued to make lazy circles on Marty's clit, their nipples rubbing briskly against each other's. "How does this feel?" she inquired softly, getting turned on herself.

"So good." Marty closed her eyes, too turned on to feel embarrassment over the fact that she was sexually responding to another woman. She spread her legs a little bit further apart, giving Ora better access to her vagina.

"Tell me when you are close to peaking, Mari." Her thumb picked up its tempo, the circles becoming more exact and demanding.

Marty gasped. She offered Ora no resistance when her mouth found hers and a tongue was thrust between her semi-parted lips. She accepted her friend's tongue, the sweetness of her breath an added turn-on to the thumb that was rubbing her wet flesh and the nipples that continued to plump up her own with their brisk rubbing.

"Well, well, well," a seductively dark voice purred out, "as fetching a scene as this makes, the deuce of you are neglecting my guests."

Marty broke away from Ora and flushed guiltily, her eyes clashing with Kil's. He looked sinfully handsome tonight, damn him any way, wearing black leather pants and a black leather vest that made his arms seem even more vein-roped and massive than they did while bare-chested.

And the way he was looking at her, the way his eyes were devouring her—*arrg!* She needed to find a way to escape this damn palace before she fell head over heels in love and lust with a man who would never love her back, a man who saw her as mere sexual chattel that he would and could do away with after he bored of her.

Well, she thought as she gritted her teeth, until she could escape she would at least try to make him jealous. If there was one thing Marty could do well, it was give as good as she got. If Kil wanted both Typpa and her and every other woman in his harem—fine. But then she would have both Death and him. And, she reminded herself, she would know by his emotions if he was affected by that fact or not.

"'Tis sorry I am, master," Ora demurred as she cast her gaze to his feet. "We will serve the sweet confections to your guests in all posthaste."

Kil's gaze flicked toward Marty. One black eyebrow arched arrogantly, as if he was waiting to hear an apology forthcoming from her lips.

Her nostrils flared. Her jaw clenched. He was crazy if he thought she'd apologize for anything. She hadn't asked for this servitude and didn't want it. If he meant to force it on her, he'd get whatever she gave to him and that was that.

Subverting the dominant paradigm, she reminded herself with a sniff. She was good at that stuff. A true aficionado.

Besides, she thought morosely, he'd let Typpa rub all over him. Pig! Nazi! Dildo breath!

—Arrg!

Kil grunted, realizing his little *heeka-beast* was more apt to blister his ears with sore words then appease him with submissive gestures. And damn the sands if he didn't grow more erect just looking at her defiant face.

His glowing blue gaze flicked hungrily over Marty once more before he turned his attention to Ora. "See that you do." And with that, he turned on his boot heel and strode from the kitchens.

Chapter Eleven

ଚୠ

Marty bit down on her lip to keep from smiling as she felt Kil's anger and jealousy building. Ignoring him completely, she carried the tray of sweet confections and fire-berries up to Lord Death, making certain she stood on the right side of him so the king would get a close up view of her flirting.

Ora had been right, she mentally conceded. When a woman is physically aroused, she does feel as though she was born to seduce.

Lord Death's dark head came up slowly, having realized for the first time that a bound servant stood beside him. His glowing gold gaze found her nipples, fixating on the nipple ring she wore for a suspended moment. At last, after several seconds had ticked by, his golden gaze flicked upward and rested on her face. "Have you something for me?" he rumbled out.

Marty could feel Kil's anger rising at the double entendre. She knew if she looked at him his jaw would be clenched and his nostrils flaring. Good.

"I do," she whispered throatily, pressing in closer so her nipples were practically touching his lips. "*Migi*-candies, fire-berries, *glatta* balls, and *prygga*." She smiled as his gaze meandered back down to her nipples. "Would you care to sample of anything, my lord?"

The warrior's rough tongue darted out and curled around the nipple that bore the blue Wani ring. Marty gasped. She hadn't been expecting that. But as she watched him sip it into his mouth, then draw from it long and leisurely with his eyes closed, she was torn between definite physical arousal from the sensation and embarrassment of being fondled in public.

And Kil—oh was he angry. And oh was his anger making her forget her embarrassment. Marty sighed lustily as she set the platter of sweets down upon the raised table, then ran her hands through Death's hair. She pressed his face in closer to her chest, her breath hitching when he began to suckle more vigorously from her nipple.

And then the warrior's hand was parting her *qi'ka* skirt, his fingers running through the honey-gold curls covering her mons. She experienced a moment's panic when his large thumb settled over her clit, but subdued it in favor of arousal—and delicious revenge.

"Mari."

Kil's voice. Low and menacing.

Marty ignored him as she closed her eyes and pressed her body closer to Death's. His lips continued to plump up and suckle from her nipple while his thumb began working in vigorous circles on her clit. She gasped, her neck baring to him.

"Mari."

Kil's voice again. Her name had been growled out warningly that time.

Marty secreted away a smile as she opened her eyes, pretending it was the first time she'd heard her name called. "I'm sorry," she said with feigned sweetness, spreading her legs further apart on the floor so Death could play with her flesh to his hearts' content, "were you speaking to me?"

A muscle began to tic in Kil's jaw. "Ye*ssss*," he hissed. His nostrils flared as his gaze flicked towards his friend. "Death," he barked, "release my bound servant that she might serve me the sweet confections."

Death's head surfaced from Marty's chest long enough to grunt. That accomplished, he buried his face in her breasts and resumed his contented suckling.

Marty raised her eyebrows to Kil challengingly. "I'm certain Typpa would be more than happy to serve you." She waved a hand about ceremoniously. "Or any other of your harem."

His hand visibly balled into a fist. "For a certainty they would," he gritted out, "yet do I command you to attend to me anon."

With a flick of his wrist to signal her, Typpa left Kil's side and strolled saucily up to Death's. Falling to her knees before him, she removed his erection from his leather pants and began to suckle on him beneath the raised table. Death groaned into Marty's breasts, offered her nipples a few more quick sips, then turned his attention to Typpa.

Marty blinked. That quickly the giant warrior had forgotten her. Apparently the rumors about warriors and their sexual attention spans were true. So why then did Kil still want her when he had so many others to service him?

Mentally shrugging, she picked up the platter of sweets and walked slowly towards the king. His anger and jealousy were such tangible things to her, she had to restrain herself from singing with triumph. Clearly she had pushed him a bit too far. Good.

Kil's menacingly narrowed eyes never left hers as he took the platter of sweets from her grasp and handed it over to a bound servant who stood behind him. After getting her first good look at his face, Marty's eyes widened a bit, never having thought he'd grow *this* agitated by her sex play with Lord Death.

And oh lord was he agitated. She could feel his rage as if it was her own.

Groovy.

"You wanted me?" she sniffed.

"Oh aye, I want you wench," he said softly, each word spoken through gritted teeth. "Now take yourself off to my bedchamber anon and await my attention there."

Marty's eyes narrowed. "No."

Kil's nostrils flared impossibly further. "You think to tell your master nay?"

Her back went rigid at his use of the word master. Pig! Nazi! Dildo breath! "I have no master," she ground out, "but I am definitely telling *you* no."

His eyebrows shot up mockingly. "Mayhap I shall take you here and now for all to see." He covered her throat with one large hand and slowly inched downwards, stopping to massage her breasts when he reached them. "Shall I taste that sweet channel of yours up on the raised table or shall I splay you on all fours and fuck you mindless?"

A tremor of guilt passed through Kil at Marty's hurt expression. He gentled his voice and leaned in closer to her that none but the two of them would bear witness to the conversation. "I *am* your master, little one, and you would do yourself a service to remember that fact." He raked her body with his gaze. "I have missed you *ty'ka*," he said hoarsely. "Let us belabor the fact of your servitude no more."

Marty gasped — partly from pleasure, partly from shock — when Kil leaned over and began flicking at her navel ring with his tongue right there for everyone to see. She moaned loudly, unable to stifle the reaction, which caused the other warriors seated around the raised table to stop what they were doing and watch her. Even the king's cousin, who had been busy fondling Ora, stopped to see what was going to happen next.

For a moment Marty was upset. But only for a moment. When her bizarre tap on Kil's emotions confirmed the fact that he was publicly touching her only because he'd missed her and not in order to show her who was boss in front of his friends, she was somehow able to let go and enjoy the wickedness of the moment, secure in the knowledge he would never let another warrior touch her.

Besides, she might not understand how a lot of things worked on Morak, but she understood enough of the culture to know that very little if anything at all was thought about public sexual displays. But oh lord, she thought as she groaned, these displays were sinfully wicked to her earthly mind and therefore gluttonously arousing.

Kil's tongue continued to flick at the navel ring as his fingers found the wet flesh between her legs and began to toy with it. He teased her clit with soft strokes, causing Marty to reach down and press his fingers harder against her. *"Please."*

He did as she wished until Marty screamed out her climax, too deliriously turned on to care what anyone thought. A moment later she was being hoisted up into the air and her *qi'ka* was being thrown to the black crystal floor. She heard him groan as he placed her on his lap, positioning her body so she straddled him.

"Put me inside of you," Kil murmured, his eyes glazed over with desire. He nipped at her bottom lip with his teeth. "I need to feel your channel, Mari."

Marty blinked. For the second time in as many days, the man had somehow rid himself of clothing without her being aware of how or when he'd done it. She could feel the tip of his erection poised at her opening, wanting enveloped within her. She discarded the thought as irrelevant, mentally filing it away as information she would find out later.

What was relevant at the moment was the fact that he wanted her to ride him right here at the raised table. As the intensity of her orgasm lessened and she once again felt normal and calm, she experienced a pang of apprehension, uncertain she could behave so wantonly in front of the other warriors and servants.

But when she glanced over her shoulder at Ora and saw that her friend was silently telling her yes, she *had* managed to inflame the king's senses, she found her courage renewed — and her resolve to keep Typpa away from him restored. That she, an avowed independent feminist, would even care to set out on such an *un*-independent course was a fact she decided to ignore altogether. For now.

Grabbing Kil's thick cock by the base, she raised her hips up and slowly, teasingly, began to envelop him within her.

He hissed at the teasing, his fingers sinking into the flesh of her hips. "'Twill be the death of me," he rasped out, "if you do not take all of me in the soonest."

Marty could feel the gaze of the other warriors on her. Knowing that they could see everything, that they were watching her naked buttocks slowly sink down on him, turned her on more than the navel ring incident had. She felt like a sex goddess.

"I don't want you to die," she said throatily so only Kil could hear. She sank down another couple of inches, giving him a bit more of her flesh. "Who else will fuck me all night long if that happens?"

His gaze clashed with hers. His jaw tightened. "No one, Mari. 'Tis best for a certainty do you realize that."

She sank down a bit further, giving him more of her pussy. For some reason, she felt the perverse need to goad him. "Then what will you do," she said saucily as she wrapped her arms around his neck, "when five Yessat years have passed and I am free to go?"

She could feel the melancholia come over him at the mere mentioning of her leaving him. Part of her said to back down, to not hurt him needlessly with her words, but her female intuition demanded that she force this warlord, a warrior who made a habit of running from his feelings, to face the fact that they shared a bizarre bond.

She could never leave him and be the same. She accepted this as fact. It didn't mean she wouldn't leave him, but she knew she'd never be the same woman when she did.

Kil, however, was resisting the idea that her leave-taking would be of import to him. His next words confirmed that fact. "It doesn't bear dwelling upon," he gritted out, clearly disliking being made to face anything he didn't want to consider, "five Yessat years is a long, long time from this moon-rising."

Marty would have been saddened by his words had she not known that his emotions were currently in turmoil. She decided to let him off the hook—for now—and allow him to deal with his need for her in the only way he understood.

Marty sank down onto his lap fully, impaling herself to the hilt. They both groaned, his fingers digging into her flesh as she began to ride up and down the length of him.

"'Tis bliss," Kil ground out, his breathing labored, "your channel is sweet bliss, little one."

She picked up the pace of her riding, moaning and groaning each time she impaled herself. When his palms found her buttocks and began kneading them, she pressed her upper body closer to his that her nipples stabbed against his chest.

"Kil."

She shouted out his name as she rode him, both of them too oblivious with lust to notice the fact that the other warriors and servants were gaping at them—not because they were mating, but because Marty had first-named her master...and he didn't seem to mind.

"Faster," he growled. He studied her face, enjoying the fact that she was so turned on she could scarcely keep her eyes open. "Ride me faster, *pani.*"

Marty complied, groaning as her flesh enveloped his. She rotated her hips and sank down on him again and again, faster and faster.

Kil's jaw clenched. His fingers dug into her buttocks as her flesh began milking his. "You think to make me spurt already, lusty one, but I will not spurt until your channel floods for me." One large hand left her buttocks in favor of flicking at her navel ring. The other hand came around and found her clit. "Come for your master," he murmured. "Come for me, Mari."

But Marty needed no further prompting. She had been close to climaxing before his fingers had started working on her, so adding them into the mix only brought it on harder and quicker. And the navel ring—

"Oh god."

Marty groaned loudly as she came, her flesh frenziedly contracting around his cock to milk him. A moment later she heard his hoarse shout of satisfaction, then felt his warm semen spurting deep inside of her.

Now that the show was over, the other warriors returned their attention to the bound servants they'd previously been fondling. Marty could hear Ora sighing lustily, which could only mean the warrior was licking and sucking on her various body parts. She secreted away a smile, happy that they'd both gotten the attention they'd sought out tonight.

Kil murmured her name, which brought Marty's attention back to him. She looked at him questioningly, her arms still wrapped around his neck, their flesh still joined.

His fingers kneaded her buttocks as his gaze clashed with hers. "I've the need to leave Morak for a spell that I might accompany Lord Death to my brother's holding on Sypar." He mentally gritted his teeth, having never explained his absences to a wench before. "I bid you to leave the harem chamber whilst I am away and move your possessions into mine."

He realized his brothers and Death would think he'd lost his mind if they ever found out about this, and mayhap he had. All he knew was that he desired—nay needed—her presence.

'Twas fact that even the four moon-risings he'd be gone away to Sypar would be hellish. He had come to realize that he would not go on the bride-quest with Rem now that Death had decided to go, for he couldn't bear to be separated so long from his bound servant and her sweet, tight channel.

Marty kissed the tip of his nose. Not even Typpa and her triple D boobs had managed to move into Kil's bedchamber.

"Okay," she said on a smile, offering him no argument. Later she would wonder at how much of an idiot she was for agreeing to make their living situation even more intimate. She was destined to fall in love with him, she knew. Which could only mean she was equally destined for heartbreak.

Kil grunted, happier than he cared to admit by her quick acceptance. He had expected a fight and she'd given him none. Yet the wench would argue with him over trifles. She was a boggle. And she had bewitched him.

"I will make it known to the warrior guardsmen who remain behind that your channel is mine and only mine." His glowing blue eyes burned possessively into her gray ones. "I will know, Mari, do you mate with another. Do not force me to punish you."

Marty's lips puckered into a frown. He'd gone from seducing her with his possessiveness to pissing her off with it by talk of punishment — and all in a second's time. "I—"

Kil pressed a finger to her lips, forestalling any arguments or blistering words she might have for him. "Keep your channel tight for me, *ty'ka*," he rumbled out warningly. "'Tis all I ask."

Chapter Twelve

ဆ

Kil left Sypar feeling surlier than a gulch beast—a condition that lasted for the next several moon-risings. He had tried to couple with his brother's bound servants whilst visiting the Ice Palace—they were lusty, busty beauties the lot of them—and yet when push came to shove, he had been unable to sustain an erection for any of them.

Yeeck! If those bedamned servants decided to talk, 'twould be more than a wee bit embarrassing for him. He, Kil Q'an Tal, unable to couple?

Well, he sniffed, at least 'twas unlikely any warriors would believe it should such blasphemous stories reach their bedamned ears.

Kil gritted his teeth as he navigated his high-speed conveyance back toward Morak. He was losing his mind for a certainty, he decided. He was losing it and what's more, it was for a certainty he'd never again find it.

The worst part was that he had lied to Rem. His own brother—he had lied to him! Confused, and too embarrassed to admit the way he felt toward his bound servant to anyone, he had invented mythical battlings in the far sectors as his reason for not leaving for the first dimension. He should have gone with him, should have gone to make certain his brother fared well, and he felt as though he was a lesser man for not having done so.

And just look where it had gotten him.

En route back to Morak from Sypar, a blood-curdling holo-call had come through, causing Kil to turn his conveyance around and head for the fifth dimension at sonic-speed. His brother had found his *nee'ka*, aye, but his gastrolight cruiser had hit a meteorite and plummeted out of control into a wormhole.

But then en route to the fifth dimension Rem himself had sent out another holo-call, advising him 'twas fruitless to come after them. Obtaining a gastrolight cruiser and hunting them down would do no good, for they were now on Joo and the planet's atmosphere was such that gastrolight cruisers could enter it but so far.

So Kil had turned around yet again, knowing he would have to wait. He would meet up with Rem at the mountains of Joo following wee Kara's come-out.

And so now — finally — he was headed back to Morak for a short spell. He had thought to venture onward to Sand City and stay there until he departed for Joo, but nay, he could not be so long removed from Mari's charms. He needed to be with her for a time, to feel her channel milking him again.

Truly, Kil did not think he deserved even this short respite. He should be on Joo with Rem, Death, and Rem's *nee'ka*. And he would have been had he not lied to his brother and friend about battling in the far sectors and gone on the bride-quest as he'd originally planned to do.

Kil's true reason for not questing with Rem and Death had been a thousand times worse than bloodshed in the far sectors, at least to Kil's way of thinking. He had simply been overwhelmed with panic at the mere thought of being removed from Mari for the length of an entire quest. Aye, he could have taken her with him into the first dimension, yet then the others would have been scrutinizing his unnatural attachment to her, mayhap even making jest of it.

Kil groaned as he ran a hand agitatedly through his hair. What in the name of the goddess Aparna was happening to him? Had he developed some rare malady that made a warrior lose his bedamned mind? Or had the Wani *mykk* given Mari some manner of potion to keep his staff hard and his man sac tight only for her? Or mayhap —

Bah! He would not think on it. He would get back to Morak the soonest and find the surcease he needed inside Mari's tight channel. He would question himself no more. 'Twas tiring for a certainty, he morosely conceded.

A picture of beautiful, beloved Mari popped into Kil's mind as he switched the high-speed conveyance down to hyper mode. He gritted his teeth when it occurred to him that the mere thought of her made his hearts swoon.

—Arrg!

* * * * *

In the middle of the night, Marty slowly awoke to the feel of Kil stroking in and out of her body from behind. She could hear his moaning and groaning, could feel the almost delirious euphoria he experienced from being inside of her. She knew that if she were on her back instead of her belly, she'd see how corded his muscles were, how tightly his jaw was clenched, how his jugular vein would bulge as his teeth gritted.

"Ah *ty'ka*," he rasped out, "I have missed you."

He needed her. He didn't want to admit it, but she knew that he did.

And she needed him. She had come to realize this as a cold hard fact during the seemingly endless days when he'd been gone. Every day, every hour, every moment, had seemed an eternity with him away.

But that didn't mean she could stay here. She couldn't and she wouldn't.

Marty wasn't the type of woman to run away from her emotions. Nor was she the type to run away from good causes—her involvement in the women's movement back on earth was proof positive of that fact.

But she also knew when she was facing insurmountable odds. Kil might need her, he might even love her, but he would never admit to either emotion. And because of that fact, she would never be more to him than a sex slave.

Ora's servitude was over in less than a month's time. When Ora left Morak and returned to her home planet, Marty would leave too and go with her. The two of them had made this decision after Marty had confided all of her feelings to her friend and Ora had insisted on helping her to escape Kil.

Marty felt tears burning in the back of her eyes at the mere thought of leaving him. But she knew it was for the best. Something deep down inside of her told her it was the only way. She could never be a docile submissive. She would never be happy in her current status as the other harem members seemed to be. Even knowing as she did that Kil hadn't had sex with any of them since he'd made love to her, it still wasn't enough. She couldn't bear the thought of being subjugated to anyone, least of all to the very man she was in love with.

"I've missed you too," she murmured. She reared up her buttocks to let him know she was awake and thoroughly enjoying his lovemaking.

Kil's hand moved underneath her. "Raise up on all fours, little one. I need to be as deep in your channel as possible."

Marty complied, coming up on her knees and elbows. He immediately sank fully into her, wringing a groan from both of them.

"'Tis tight," he gritted out as he began his rhythm and stroked quickly in and out of her, "and 'tis mine."

He mated her hard, rode her body as though he'd never get enough of it, which he feared was true. Her breasts jiggled beneath her at the hard pummeling he gave her, and he couldn't resist reaching down to tweak her nipples whilst he rode her into a place better than oblivion.

Marty took all of him, wanting everything he could give to her. She couldn't stifle the tremors of sadness that passed through her at knowing she was leaving him, so she decided to make the most of this time with him while she had it.

"I love you, Kil," she whispered.

She bit down hard on her lip to keep from crying when he said nothing back.

* * * * *

For the next three days, Kil did not allow Mari to leave his sight. They made love hour after hour, time and time again, in every way imaginable.

He had taken her into his bathing chamber and watched the *Kefas* bring her to climax, then made love to her himself. He had bade Ora to come to his bedchamber, then watched as she and Marty had kissed and fondled each other. Afterwards he had been so hard, he'd found it necessary to mount Marty four times before he'd felt replete.

But mostly, Kil made love to her alone, with no *Kefa* or bound servant present to witness their matings. 'Twas as he preferred it and that in and of itself was powerfully frightening.

But the most frightening aspect of it all was the desire he felt to be with her at all times, regardless to whether or not he was mating with her. He wanted to...talk to her. He enjoyed listening to her stories of earth and found himself willing to tell her things he'd never confided to another.

He wanted to...be with her. He found himself happy just having her nearness, just knowing she was there and was his.

And she had told him that she loved him. As crazed as it sounded—a lasting union between a king and his harem's favored—he was beginning to wonder if mayhap he too...

Bah—he could not think on it. Yet he realized that he needed to think on it, and fast.

He knew—*knew*—that the ice within him was melting where she was concerned, that a primal part of him was banging at his hearts screaming to get out.

He needed to think.

He needed to battle.

And so on the fourth day when Kil heard tell of possible trouble brewing in the far sectors, he left Morak with all speed. He tried to harden his hearts at the pain he knew Mari was feeling when he left her, but he couldn't.

Mayhap because he felt it too.

Chapter Thirteen

ജ

Over the course of the next few weeks, he had gone to her on one last occasion. For the rest of the time he had stayed away, seeking battles where they didn't exist, attending wee Kara's come-out, rescuing a brother who no longer needed him...

But after he'd returned from Joo, Kil hadn't been able to stave off the need to see Mari. And so he had gone to her and, just as she always did, she had held out her arms to him and offered his body and hearts surcease with the use of her lovemaking. He had come down on top of her with a groan, feeling like a wounded warrior who had at last found a healing elixir.

Seated in the dining hall within the ice-jewel walls of the Ice Palace with the rest of his family, Kil drank of his *matpow* as he reminisced o'er the last eve he had spent with wee Mari.

Their mating had been wild that moon-rising, he remembered. She had been as desperate to feel him inside of her as he had been to be there. For once it had been Mari who had been the aggressor, straddling his hips and riding him hard over and over again throughout the eve. She had taken him into her channel more times than he could count, loving his body with hers until the subverted yellow sun streaked through the crimson red night and declared it morn.

She had told him that she loved him. Over and over again she had whispered the words until even he had believed them. He had opened his mouth to give the love words back, but had nigh unto panicked trying to get them out. Kil Q'an Tal had never said such words to another being. Not once in all of his hundreds of years of existence.

102

As if she had understood, Mari had not pressed the issue, had instead continued to sink her channel down onto his shaft as she kept saying the love words to him over and over again, never expecting them to be returned.

'Twas as if she had thought never to see him again and therefore needed to say what lay in her heart as much as was possible. But nay...

Kil frowned into his goblet as his eyes flicked about the dining hall. His entire family was here, celebrating the addition of Giselle into the family, along with her and Rem's tiny hatchlings. Everyone was happy, everyone was making merry, and yet here he sat brooding into his goblet.

He had been removed from Mari for nigh unto a fortnight. And on that last wondrous eve when she had given her body and heart to him so completely, he had all but thrown the gifts back in her face, too stubborn and afraid to give her all of him in return.

And truly, what was his fear? That his brothers would make jest that he'd been bewitched by his own bound servant?

Nay. When all was said and done, Kil was a warrior who marched to no one's tune but his own. They could laugh and make jest and at this point he was too far intoxicated with Mari to care.

So what was the real reason? Why the panic and fear? Until he could answer that question...

"I apologize brothers," Kil said as he raised his goblet of *matpow* to his lips, "but I fear I must leave this moon-rising to see to my sectors."

Zor raised an eyebrow. "You've been seeing to your sectors a lot as of late. I hope there is naught amiss?"

Ah, but there is plenty amiss. Your foolish brother cannot stand to be separated from his own bedeviling bound servant. "Nay," Kil murmured, "naught is amiss."

Foolish. Was he foolish for being bedeviled, or foolish for not admitting that he was bedeviled to Mari? He hoped it was the former, but strongly suspected it was the latter.

Kil's entire body stilled as an odd premonition passed through him.

Mari.

He needed to get back to Mari. Something was…very wrong.

* * * * *

She was gone. She had run away.

Bellowing like a madman, Kil's fist came crashing down upon the closest tabletop, shattering the crystal structure into a million pieces.

She had left him. She had dared to escape him whilst he'd been away.

Barking at one of his warriors to prepare a high-speed conveyance for his departure, Kil's heavy footfalls could be heard throughout the palace corridor as he made his way to the launching pad.

If she thought she could escape him, he told himself grimly, then she had better think again. He would find her. He had a lock on her scent.

The scar on his cheek twisted in rage as he alighted into his high-speed conveyance. In the midst of his fury it never dawned on the King of Morak that there was a reason he was able to get a lock on her scent to begin with. All he knew was that he had to have her back. And he had to have her anon.

King Kil Q'an Tal, the most feared and ruthless warlord that the time dimensions had ever known, launched from the conveyance pad preparing to do what it was he did best. He was preparing to hunt. The only difference, he thought as his jaw clenched unforgivingly, was that this time what he hunted was a wench.

* * * * *

She accepted the bag of credits from the tradesman who had offered her a high price for one of her *qi'kas*. Glancing over her shoulder to make certain she wasn't being followed, she fled into the busy village and made her way towards the tiny crystal shack she was hiding out in.

She stopped for a moment as a strange flutter quivered through her belly. That was the second time in as many weeks. Reminding herself that she had no time to ponder the foreign sensation, she walked briskly into the village centre, her scent mingling as one with the other passersby.

Chapter Fourteen
The Vakki Sector of Planet Zolak
Trek Mi Q'an Galaxy, Seventh Dimension

ഇ

"Thank the goddess," Ora breathed out when Marty opened up the crystal door and made her way into the tiny shack they were sharing, "I was beginning to fear the worst."

Marty's lips puckered into a frown. "No offense to your hometown, Ora, but this sector *is* the worst." She shook her head and sighed. "The entire planet is a hole. Who did you say is the ruler here?"

She smiled wryly. "King Jun, the mast—uh, the King of Morak's two-year-old nephew."

"That explains a lot," Marty mumbled. "The kid is too young to know he's inherited the planetary version of a practical joke."

Ora sighed as she walked over to a window and stared outside. "I fear I agree. 'Tis not as I remember it when first I was captured in battle five Yessat years past."

Marty crossed her arms under her breasts and listened intently. "It was Kil who captured you?"

Ora nodded, but didn't turn away from the window. "Aye. Insurrectionists plagued us for months before he came and put down the rebellion. I could have told him the truth, that I was a Zolakian and not a rebel sympathizer, yet my parents had been killed, our crops had been thieved, and I had nowhere else to go." She sighed. "So I said nothing. I was alone and I was starving, but I had my beauty."

Marty nodded. On a scale of one to ten, Ora's beauty rated somewhere around twenty. "So you let him take you away to Morak and put you in his harem."

"Aye." Ora turned around at last and smiled, if a bit sadly. "I don't regret the decision, Mari. Not even in retrospect."

Marty smiled gently. "I don't blame you. It's all any of us can do, Ora, just make the best decision we can based upon the knowledge we have at the time."

"The same as you do now," Ora murmured. She shook her head and turned back toward the window. "I apologize. 'Twas not necessary to remind you of the mast—of him."

Marty chuckled as she strolled over to where Ora stood gazing out into the black night. "As if I won't think about him if you don't mention him." She took Ora's hand in hers. "I'm just lucky I had your friendship, as well as your help to escape."

Ora squeezed her hand. "And then I brought you here to this joke known as planet Zolak." She sighed. "We really must continue on, Mari. 'Tis nothing here for either of us," she said sadly.

Marty felt as though there would be nothing for her anywhere, but she didn't say as much. She missed Kil—oh god how she missed him—but she could not and would not go back to being his sex slave. She had aimed for all or nothing and had gotten nothing. It had been the right time to leave.

"How true," Marty said quietly. She fingered the see through genie-like top she was wearing. "They can't even spin a decent *qi'ka* here."

Ora snorted at that. "Nay, they cannot." She thought things over for a moment then said, "We've plenty of credits between us. We can move on to wherever the spirit takes us."

Marty smiled, thinking back on the summer she'd backpacked through Europe. Ora would have made a decent hippie. "Have you heard of any planets in any of the galaxies where the women are not subjugated to the men?"

"Besides the Wani of Tron?"

Marty inclined her head. She knew she could never go back there. It would put her friends in danger of another war if Kil decided to try and find her and place her back within the harem. "Yes, besides the Wani."

"I can think of only one."

"Oh? And what's the planet's name?"

"Galis," she sighed.

Marty's brow furrowed. "You say that as if you don't want to go there."

"Nay, it isn't that."

"Then what's wrong?" Marty said quietly. "Why are you so upset? And don't bother denying it because I know you too well to believe it."

Ora smiled as she stared out the window. "Aye, you do. For which I am grateful. It means we are great friends."

"Then why the melancholia?"

Ora shook her head, but said nothing. She merely continued to stare out the window.

Marty turned her head and glanced out the window Ora was staring out of. She sighed when she realized why her dear friend was so upset. How could she have been so thoughtless? "This must be hard on you," she murmured. "To return to your homeland only to realize that there is nothing here for you anymore."

Ora swiped away a rogue tear. "For five Yessat years I carried this fantasy in my hearts that when I returned all would be as it had been before the insurrectionists burned my sector to the ground." She shook her head. "But time has stood still, Mari. This once beautiful land is as horrid as the day my family's holdings were first besieged."

"I'm sorry," Marty said softly.

By the time Ora turned to her, her tears were flowing freely. Her eyes searched Marty's face. "I need you to hold me tonight, Mari," she whispered.

Marty smiled gently. Ora was so beautiful, she thought. So kind, generous, and beautiful. And she wasn't the only one who needed to be loved tonight.

As if on instinct, their lips found each other. Marty ran her hands over Ora's breasts while they kissed, slowly massaging her nipples as their tongues leisurely stroked each other. They kissed for a long time, sensuous, drugging kisses that heightened into heady desire. And odd as it was, it felt right. Marty experienced none of the guilt those back on earth would have thought she should have experienced.

Some time later, Marty raised her head. "You taste like honey," she murmured.

Ora grinned. "There are other parts of me that taste better."

Marty felt a bit wicked as she watched Ora shed her *qi'ka*, realizing as she did that she found her body arousing. But then, she had come to enjoy being wicked since leaving earth.

When both of them were naked, she followed Ora to the small bed they shared and kissed her body from head to toe. She had been right. There were parts of her that tasted better than honey.

* * * * *

"Mighty One."

High Lord Jek Q'an Ri cleared his throat when 'twas apparent the king had not heard him. "Mighty One," he said a bit louder.

Kil grunted to acknowledge he had heard his paternal cousin, but did not turn from his standing position to look upon him.

"We have hunted for two days, cousin, yet she has eluded us. You've hundreds more wenches within your harem. Can we not return to Morak that we might resume instruction in the warring arts?" His eyebrows rose fractionally. "'Tis why my sire sent me to you in the first, to learn from the best."

"I know she was here," he muttered, ignoring Jek's subtle reprimand. He was of no mind to be reminded of his duties. His entire life had been naught but a duty. Should he desire to take a break from it that he might locate Mari, 'twas his business and no other's. "I can smell her perfume." He looked around the abandoned crystal shack for any telltale signs of where she might have gone, but could find no answers.

Jek squinted at that. "I do not recall her wearing a perfume."

"Do you not?" Kil glanced toward his cousin before crouching down to his knees to inspect the area under the bed. "Then mayhap you need instruction in the senses rather than in the warring arts for there is no scent in the galaxies more fine than Mari's."

Jek was about to let that go when he recalled an incident he'd overheard in the Palace of Mirrors a time ago. "Nay, Mighty One, 'tis for a certainty Mari wears no perfume." He shrugged absently. "I remember hearing her decline Ora's offering of a Zolakian perfume, claiming she broke out in red spots from the stuff."

"Then how is it possible that I can smell her—"

Kil's entire body stilled. His hearts rate plummeted, then shot up and worked triple time. By the sands—oh *Mari*. He sat there crouched on his knees for what felt an eternity before his rounded eyes shot wildly toward his cousin. "—scent," he finished softly.

Jek closed his eyes briefly and sighed. "Thank the goddess."

Kil stared open-mouthed at him for a moment before he found his voice. "Thank the goddess?" he bellowed. "'Tis

110

sorely apparent I was fool enough to place my own Sacred Mate within a harem for the love of the sands!—an unforgivable transgression for which she has escaped me—and to this you say naught but *thank the goddess?*"

Jek had the good grace to blush at that. "'Twas not why I was thanking her, Mighty One."

"Then why?" he growled, alighting to his feet.

"'Twas my fear you were becoming…touched in the head." He clapped a hand to his forehead and groaned. "Thank the goddess 'tis just a malady of the hearts brought on by repeated separation from your *nee*—"

"Touched in the head?"

Jek sighed, realizing as he did that there was no graceful exit from such a statement. "You, uh, have been…different as of late."

Kil grunted. He feared to hear the answer, but decided to ask the question any way. "How so?"

Jek had no trouble ticking off a list. In fact, Kil thought with a glower, he seemed to take great joy in the doing. "Well for starters, you have coupled with none but Mari for as long as you have owned her."

Kil's teeth clicked shut. He grunted. "Cannot a warrior be possessed of the headache without ridicule?"

Jek held up a second finger and plowed onwards. "One of Rem's bound servants let it be known that…"

Kil whimpered, dreading the telling.

"…your man staff would not—"

"*Alright.*" Kil slashed a hand tersely through the air. "I had imbibed of much *matpow* that eve. Let us belabor the point no more."

Jek held up a third finger.

Kil winced.

"And then there is the undeniable fact that as of late you have been…" His nose wrinkled in distaste. "…*nice.*"

Nice? *Arrg!* "I am never nice," Kil huffed. "Leastways," he sniffed, "is it against the Holy Law to show a kindness to one's underlings?"

"Nay, but you have also shown a kindness to our enemies—"

"When?" he gritted out. "How?"

Jek inclined his head. "When we were battling in the far sectors and won, you took none of the enemy's wenches into your harem."

"I had the headache," he gritted out. "By the sands, cannot a warrior be possessed of the headache!" His hand slashed through the air again. "'Tis for a certainty I can out-couple any warrior alive should I desire it."

Jek held up a fourth finger.

"Bah!" Kil spat. "Put down your bedamned finger before I break it off for you." His eyes narrowed menacingly. "You make it sound as though I was spotted skipping through *trelli* fields with *joo-joo* flowers woven into my hair." His jaw clenched. "So I refused a few couplings here and there. Now we know the why of it."

Jek nodded sincerely. "'Twas why I was thanking the goddess, Mighty One."

—*Arrg!* "Fine. Let us belabor the point no more." His nostrils flared. "I need to hunt down my *heeka-beast* of a *nee'ka.*"

Jek chuckled. "Shall we scout the nests in Koror?"

Kil found his first grin since realizing Mari had fled from him. "'Twill be the second place we look."

"And the first?"

Kil stopped smiling as he pondered the matter over. His first guess would be that Mari had fled back to the Wani. But nay, after he considered it further he knew she would never do anything that might put her adoptive clan in harm's way. She was thoughtful that way. Luckily his connection to her, a connection he now understood the reason behind, ensured that he could second-guess her movements better than any other.

"My *heeka-beast* will go to where she feels most at home..."

Jek nodded, the grim features that looked so much like Kil's softening a bit as he grinned. "Mayhap to a place where the pigs hold no power and the paradigms have been subverted."

Kil grinned back.

They looked at each other and smiled, then said simultaneously, "Galis."

Chapter Fifteen

Meanwhile, on the green moon of Ti Q'won...

❦

"'Tis many thanks I give to you, Auntie, for allowing me to stay here with Jana for a spell." Seated at the royal raised table in the dining hall, High Princess Kara Q'ana Tal smiled affectionately at her aunt, Queen Geris.

Geris grinned. "We're glad to have you here. Aren't we Dak?"

"For a certainty," the king said between bites of his stew. He summoned himself a piece of *maga* bread. "'Twas sporting of your future Sacred Mate to allow you to leave Sand City and visit with us for a time."

Kara's smiled faltered at the mention of High Lord Cam K'al Ra. "Aye," she said weakly, "sporting."

Princess Jana, as golden as her sire, immediately changed the subject. "*Mani*," she said, her glowing blue eyes finding her mother's brown ones, "mayhap Kara, Dari, and I can visit the shopping stalls on the morrow?"

Geris smiled. "Sure, baby. I don't see why not."

"So long as you take the warrior guardsmen," Dak announced. "Or your brother Dar."

"Aye, papa." Jana glanced from her father to Kara, then back to her mother. "May we be excused, *mani*?"

Geris' lips puckered into a frown. "But you've hardly eaten, baby."

Jana smiled, a bit nervously to Dar's way of thinking for he raised a golden eyebrow whilst he watched her trip over her tongue. "M-Mayhap we can finish eating in my bedchamber?" she asked.

Geris glanced toward Dak. When he didn't say anything, she shrugged her shoulders. "Fine. Go on then."

"Thank-you, *mani*."

Jana, Kara, and Dari scurried to stand up at the same time. Each of them picked up a platter, stopped briefly at the king and queen's sides to place a kiss on their cheeks, and hightailed it out of the dining hall.

Dar watched them make their exit through curious eyes. He turned to his mother. "I shall accompany them to the shopping stalls on the morrow, *mani*. Have you the desire to go as well?"

Geris picked up a slice of the *maga* bread and shook her head. "It sounds fun, sweetheart, but your Aunt Kyra has challenged me to a game of holo-maze." She harrumphed. "Time to win back them damn fifty credits," she mumbled under her breath.

Dar grinned, a dimple popping out onto his cheek. "You and Auntie take your holo-mazing seriously."

Dak snorted at that. "'Tis the understatement of this millennium."

Geris frowned at her husband, then turned to her son and ruffled his golden blonde hair affectionately. "Keep a good eye on the girls, baby." She sighed, her demeanor growing serious. "Especially Dari and Kara. They worry me."

Dar nodded, though he thought to himself that Jana needed watched over as closely as the other two. Dari and Kara were mischief-makers, aye, but Jana was just as wily. "For a certainty," he murmured.

Chapter Sixteen
Crystal City on Planet Galis
Trek Mi Q'an Galaxy, Seventh Dimension

∞

Marty and Ora could only gawk at their new surroundings. The rumors concerning Galis had indeed been true. This Jupiter-sized planet which sat nestled in between Zolak, which was roughly the same size, and Tryston, which was ten times bigger, was an avowed independent feminist's dream come true.

Here, as with the Wani, women ruled all facets of government and trade. Unlike the males of Wani, however, the men of Galis weren't treated harshly and given few rights. They had the say-so to make their own decisions and choose their own life-courses, it was just that the vast majority of them were content to let the women warriors rule over them.

Unlike the Wani of Tron, the female warriors of Galis were not disproportionately huge in comparison to their males. On the contrary, they were a bit smaller. The average Galis male stood about six feet in height, while the average Galis female stood approximately two to three inches shorter. In other words, the women of the planet were about the size of tall earth women, except for the fact that their bodies tended to be better honed and they sported sleek, sexy muscles.

Marty hated to admit it, but after having shared the bed of a seven and a half foot warlord who probably weighed in the vicinity of four hundred plus pounds, the males of Galis appeared rather weak and ordinary in comparison to him. Of course, it didn't help matters much that they tended to be on the emotional side, prone towards pouting when their women didn't give them their way, and sometimes even breaking out into bouts of tears if they were scolded by them.

Marty harrumphed. Definitely not groovy.

"'Tis like the realm of the goddess, is it not?" Ora whispered out the question as she gaped upwards at the beautiful white crystal high-rise structure that was to be their new home.

"Yeah, it is." Marty grinned as she glanced down at the palm of her hand. "The suite keeper said all we have to do is place our palms on the front door of our new apartm—er— suite, and the recognition scanner within it will recognize our prints and let us in." She shook her head in awe, having been catapulted from earth long before such things had ever been dreamed up let alone concocted. "It's truly amazing."

Ora shrugged, having known such technology all of her life. She was in awe of the planet itself for the beauty, wealth, and technology of the place were the stuff of legends. "I am fair bursting with excitement to see our new quarters, Mari." She jumped up and down a bit, her breasts jiggling with the movements. "Shall we go inside now, or mayhap you would prefer to dine at one of the stalls first?"

"I am hungry," Marty admitted, "but I'd really like to go upstairs and see our new place before we eat." She shuddered. "Our suite, however, is on the hundredth floor. This should be one hell of a long elevator ride."

"Elevator?" Ora's brow furrowed. "I know not your meaning, yet will the transport lift us instantaneously. 'Twill take but the blink of an eye and we will find ourselves spit out on the hundredth floor."

Marty's jaw dropped open. "You're kidding!"

"Nay." Ora giggled. "Your earth must be nigh unto primitive."

Marty agreed. In comparison it was. "Let's go on up then. I want to see it before we eat and I'm starving."

As Marty strolled arm-in-arm with Ora to the transport situated on the outside of the white crystal high-rise, she adamantly reminded herself that she absolutely did not miss Kil. She refused to consider the fact that finding it necessary to remind herself that she didn't miss him was telling unto itself.

* * * * *

Marty pressed a hand to her belly when another strange flutter went through it. Ignoring the sensation, she allowed Ora to lead her into an elegant dining stall that was draped with shimmering gold material similar to a *qi'ka*.

On Galis, women did not wear *qi'kas*—the one planetary exception in the entire galaxy of Trek Mi Q'an, she'd been told. Ora had explained to Marty that the emperor allowed them to continue on with their native dress because the Galians were law-abiding citizens who harbored a distinct dislike of insurrectionists as strongly as the warriors of Trek Mi Q'an did.

So the Galians wore what they would, their leaders content to answer to an emperor who stayed put out of their day-to-day living. Traditional Galian dress, however, was just as scandalous in its own right as a *qi'ka*. In fact, the *zoka* was made up of even less material than the *qi'ka* of a free woman, consisting of nothing more than a see through gee-string and criss-cross sandals that tied at the back of the knee. Breasts were left naked, as there was no top portion to the *zoka*.

The *zoka* Marty wore this evening was a shimmering aqua thong with gold sandals, two colors that contrasted well against her lightly tanned skin. Ora looked equally fetching in a silver thong with maroon sandals.

Marty stifled a tremor of giddiness as she and Ora sauntered into the eating establishment. Sometimes it still amazed her that she, Marty Mathews, had somehow managed to catapult from earth to live in what was now her fourth alien civilization. Absolutely astounding.

Equally amazing was the fact that she was so used to walking around with her breasts jiggling to and fro, that it no longer bothered her to have men stare at them, clearly desiring her. In fact, watching men stare at her naked breasts, as a few patrons in the dining stall were currently doing, was definitely arousing. Not arousing in the sense that she wanted to have sexual relations with the men, but physically arousing in the sense that it turned her on to be stared at and sexually coveted by them.

"Ooohh," Ora whispered as the women took their seats on the *vesha* pad they'd been escorted to, "these pads feel much like the harem pillows, do they not?"

Marty flinched as if she'd been struck, the reminder of the king she'd left behind unexpectedly upsetting.

"Oh goddess," Ora said in the way of apology, "'tis sorry I am to have—"

"Forget it." Marty smiled as she settled her body down and propped herself up on her left elbow. "Really."

Ora propped herself up on her right elbow so that they were lying face to face across from each other. She sighed. "I keep putting my foot in my mouth, I fear..."

She broke off from speaking when a naked serving wench strolled over to their pad and kneeled down to place a long golden trencher in between them. The serving wench, a beautiful redhead with pearly, porcelain skin, smiled at them. "There's enough food here to feed four," she offered in Trystonni. "Enjoy."

Marty smiled. "We will. Thanks."

The serving wench inclined her head, then stood up to leave. "Press the holo-button at the head of the trencher if you need me."

Ora cocked her head as she studied her. Her eyes narrowed speculatively. "You seem familiar to me. Were you ever placed within a harem?"

The redhead grinned. "No, can't say that I was." She stood up, which drew the women's gaze to the trimmed thatch of wine-red curls between her thighs. "Lots of people say that to me, though. That I seem familiar to them, I mean." She shrugged.

"Oh well," Ora said, shrugging her own shoulders, "you mayhap have one of those faces then."

"Perhaps." The redhead smiled down to them before leaving. "If you need anything, just holler."

Marty nodded. "What's your name by the way?"

"Kara, but to be honest nobody has called me that in years." She grinned, causing a dimple to pop out on either cheek. "When I first arrived on Galis the women christened me Kari."

"Ahh." Marty understood all about that. She grinned back. "They couldn't pronounce your name I take it?"

"Something like that." Kari pointed to the wine-red hair cascading down her back. "But mostly they named me Kari because of the color of my hair."

"What does *Kari* mean in Galian?"

"Fire-berry."

* * * * *

Kil's nostrils flared as Mari's scent filled them. He was close, he knew. Very, very close.

Methodically, his gaze flicked about the main street of Crystal City. To the east, to the west—back to the east. His eyes narrowed. "I detect the scent of her arousal," he murmured.

Jek's eyebrows rose fractionally. "Which way did she go?"

Kil's jaw clenched. If Mari had dared to give her channel to another male, even a lesser male, he would not be responsible for his actions. "East," he growled.

* * * * *

"Wow."

Marty chuckled softly as she and Ora watched Kari perform a very tantalizing strip tease for the viewing pleasure of the warriors who had come to Crystal City either on trading business or just to see what the legendary planet was like. The warriors whistled and catcalled, all of them worked up into sexual need watching the beautiful redhead perform.

Ora giggled. "The warriors lounged about are nigh unto bursting."

"Uh huh." Still propped up on her left elbow, Marty grinned as she glanced up at the stage. "I had no idea the servers here put on shows as well."

Ora nodded. "Galis is where the erotic arts first began thousands of Yessat years past. The wenches of these sectors are the most skilled in the galaxies for they study the art of peaking for many, many years before they become full-time performers."

Marty shook her head and smiled wryly. The art of peaking indeed. "So Kari is still a student then?"

"Aye. When her mistress feels she is fully trained she will practice the erotic arts as a full-time craft. Until then..." She shrugged. "An apprentice still has bills to pay."

"Hence the trencher-serving bit."

"Aye."

Marty's brow wrinkled in thought. "What exactly is the art of peaking?"

Ora looked at her as though she'd lost her mind.

Marty rolled her eyes. "I know what peaking is, Ora. I mean how exactly do these erotic arts performers make it a—well, an art?"

"Oh that." She sighed. "I wish I knew how 'tis they do what they do, but the Galian wenches are very secretive about their craft."

"But what is it that they do?" She threw a hand toward the stage. "Kari's little performance is hot and all, but she's not doing anything unexplainable."

"Ah but the show is not yet over," Ora murmured. "Watch for yourself and witness the art of peaking."

Marty gave up and watched in silence, realizing as she did that Ora would not be forthcoming with information. Her friend wanted her to be surprised, so surprised she supposed she'd have to be.

One thing Marty had to hand to Kari was her ability to put on a good show. Her movements were graceful, agile, a woman who for all appearances had been born to seduce. The way she slowly strode across the stage with confidence, the way she rubbed her hands all over her body as though it was made of the finest silk—everything she did was sexy and arousing.

And then Kari was settling herself before a table of warriors on a crystal chair-like mechanism. She spread her thighs wide, ran the fingers of one hand slowly through her thatch of wine-red curls, then lower to massage her labia and clit. The warriors' mouths seemed to water as they watched her, all of them desiring to thrust inside of her.

But to Marty's surprise, Kari didn't invite any of them to thrust inside of her. Marty had half-expected that mating with the warriors would be part of the Galian show. But no, to Marty's delight Kari allowed but one warrior to approach her, and even he was offered no pleasure. Instead, he was offered the chance to pleasure *her*. Marty found herself giggling.

Ora turned her head long enough to grin at Marty. "Role reversal, aye?" She giggled. "I love it."

"Me too."

Marty's entire experience with warriors had been one of watching them take their own pleasure with bound servants where they would. It wasn't that they provided no climax to the bound servants for they provided them with climaxes left and right, but clearly the hunters in Kil's employ had always thought of their own pleasure first rather than the pleasure of the one pleasing them. Kari's little show was definitely novel.

Not to mention arousing.

Marty felt her eyes glazing over and her nipples hardening as she watched an attractive black-haired warrior slither his tongue around Kari's labial folds. Kari shivered and sighed, her pink nipples stabbing upward from puffy areolas.

The warrior groaned. In fact, oddly enough, all of the warriors watching groaned too.

Surprised, Marty glanced around trying to figure out what was going on. But she was so hot and bothered, so close to peaking that…

"Oh god."

Marty moaned when it dawned on her exactly what Kari was able to do. She was able to transfer her arousal to every patron in the dining stall, making all of them feel the same arousal she felt. When Kari peaked, *all* of them would peak.

"How groovy," Marty groaned.

Ora turned her head a moment to look at Marty. Her expression said she was torn between the impending need to climax and the need to giggle. Climaxing won out. "'Tis groovy for a certainty," Ora said on a moan, her nipples stabbing upward and her eyes closing as climax approached faster and faster.

Through a haze of passion, Marty's gaze meandered up to the stage to watch Kari. The performer's moans and groans came louder and faster as the warrior buried his face between her legs and lapped at her. Marty's view was so close she could hear the warrior's throaty growl, could see his lips sipping in her clit and suckling it.

Kari's body began to convulse.

The audience moaned.

Kari's hands found her nipples and tweaked them as her breathing grew more and more labored.

The audience groaned.

Kari screamed as she came, her entire body shuddering and convulsing.

Marty rolled onto her back with a lusty moan, her eyes closed in bliss as her thighs spread wide and she came violently. *"Oh god."*

She had no time to register the fact that her *zoka* had mysteriously disappeared, for within a second's time she was given two new oddities to consider: a necklace had been clasped about her neck and a long, thick cock was sliding inside of her.

Marty's eyes flew open on a gasp, then widened when she saw who it was thrusting inside of her. "Kil," she groaned, her legs instinctively wrapping around his waist.

She should have been worried, should have tried to somehow disjoin their bodies so she could flee, but she was so physically aroused, and she had missed him so damn much. Later she would deal with things. Later she would tell him that she would never return to Morak as a slave. But for now...

"Ah *nee'ka*," he said hoarsely as he slid himself in to the hilt, "I have missed you sorely."

Marty's eyes widened. Her hand flew up to grasp the necklace about her neck, the one he was no longer wearing. *Nee'ka*. He had called her...

"Aye," Kil murmured as he placed a large palm at either side of her head and stilled, "I have made you my wife." His glowing blue gaze found her gray one and for the first time since she'd known him he looked distraught and unsure of himself. "What think you of that?" he asked arrogantly, though she could feel his vulnerability.

"I don't know," Marty said quietly, honestly. "What should I think?"

Kil flinched as though he'd been wounded. "'Tis sorry I am," he said hoarsely, "for being too much the fool to recognize my own Sacred Mate upon seeing her." His eyes dimmed a bit, which tugged at Marty's heartstrings. "Mayhap you will forgive me one day?"

Marty studied his features. She knew he was in agony, but she needed things settled once and for all. "And if I don't?"

He sucked in his breath, making her feel like a lecher, but she didn't back down. "Then I will keep you any way," he murmured in a wounded voice.

She refused to be moved. It was time to settle things once and for all or she'd fight him every step of the way. "You need me so much that you would keep me even if I didn't want to be with you? Even if I hated you?"

Kil closed his eyes briefly, as if in pain. "I would that I could change your loathing of me, but aye," he rasped out, "I will keep you no matter what."

"Why?" It was now or never, her mind screamed out. Now or never. "Tell me why."

His nostrils flared. She could tell that he didn't want to be pushed into giving all of himself over to her, yet she would accept nothing less. All or nothing.

"Why?" she asked again, her own nostrils doing a bit of flaring. "Why do you need me that much?" When he only stared down at her but made no move to speak, she began pushing at his immovable wall of a chest. "Let me up, Kil. I'm not going back to Morak with you."

"Then I will force you to come," he gritted out. "I own you by the Holy Law. You are my Sacred Mate."

Her eyes narrowed. "Yes, you can force me, and yes, I know there isn't a damn thing I can do to stop you. But I'm telling you now that your entire life will be one big chase because I will run from you at every opportunity. Do you really want that?"

"Do not do this thing to us, *nee'ka*," he said hoarsely. "Please...do not."

Marty closed her eyes briefly and sighed. "I'm not doing anything to us, Kil," she whispered in a defeated tone. "That honor belongs to you."

He sucked in his breath, affronted. "Do not say that."

"It's true." She shook her head sadly. "I offered you all of me, but you gave me only a part of you in return. You don't want me to get too close..." Her voice trailed off as a strange fatigue began to come over her. She blinked it away and plowed on. "You want to keep me at arm's length. And I cannot—will not—live a life with you like that."

The muscles in his entire body tensed. "What do you want from me?" he ground out.

She met his gaze unflinchingly. "Everything."

Kil's body stilled. Everything. She wanted everything.

His eyes flicked about her face as he studied her features, completely amazed and humbled by this wee woman. She had lived through so much in these past months, things many if not most would never have been able to overcome by the sheer force of their will. She had been thrust from one major life change to the next and faced all of them proud and unscathed. She was strong and determined. And she loved him. In that moment he understood why it was that she had been born to complete him. And why it was that no other woman ever could.

"Then you have it, little warrior." His words were soft, but certain. "I give you everything."

Marty's eyes rounded. She blinked back tears. "Do you mean that?" she whispered.

"Aye." Kil smiled slowly as his gaze locked with hers. "Aye, I do."

Marty intertwined her legs with his as she smiled from ear to ear. She grabbed his buttocks and kneaded them with her fingers. He might not be ready to say the love words she wanted to hear, but she knew with all of her heart that he felt them. For the first time she was completely certain, and for now just knowing that he loved her was enough. She'd give him, oh a week or two to fess up. "And the harem?"

"Gone," he groaned.

"And you'll buy us a second estate on Galis?" She knew she was pushing her luck, but she really liked it here.

Kil grunted. "If it means your forgiveness, I will conquer the entire bedamned planet and hand it to you as a bride gift."

She giggled, totally enjoying his need to appease her. "What a groovy thing to say, but completely unnecessary. A suite here will do."

"'Tis done."

"What about—"

"*Nee'ka,*" he growled. "I will like as naught die if you do not milk me with your channel the soonest. It has been an eternity since I last sampled of your charms."

Marty grinned as she continued to knead his buttocks. "Then quit going off looking for wars."

Kil repositioned himself so he could fling her legs over his shoulders. "I will never separate from you again." His gaze met hers as he slid deeply inside of her. "Never."

Marty gasped, no longer in the mood to talk. "Groovy," she groaned.

"Mari," he rasped out as he slid into her over and over again, "when you left me I wanted to die." He held on to her thighs and stroked into her flesh to the core. His hips slowly rotated back and forth, his shaft grinding into her. "You are mine, *ty'ka.* Forever mine."

And then neither of them was in the mood to talk for his body was possessing hers fully, thrusting in and out of her as though he meant to brand her. He rode her hard, the sound of her flesh enveloping his, the musky scent of their arousal, as intoxicating as the mating ritual itself.

"Kil."

Marty closed her eyes and groaned, her hips slamming up to meet each of his thrusts. Kil reached in between them and plucked at her nipples while he rode her, pounding into her as he plumped them.

"Milk me," he said hoarsely. "Come for your husband, Mari."

His other hand found her navel ring and he flicked it back and forth, his cock thrusting into her flesh frenziedly, over and over, again and again.

"Oh god."

Marty arched her back as she wrapped her legs tightly around his neck. *"Harder,"* she groaned. *"Fuck me harder."*

Kil gritted his teeth as he complied, his jugular vein bulging as he sank into her flesh deeper and harder. "Come," he commanded her, his tight balls slapping against her buttocks. "Come for me, little one."

"I love you."

Marty groaned out the love words as her back arched, her breasts thrust skyward, and she came. Moaning, she continued to rock her hips, meeting each of his thrusts as blood rushed to her face and nipples. *"Yes."*

Kil mounted her hard, riding her into oblivion. He opened his mouth to give the love words back as he thrust into her flesh, but a relentless orgasm tore through him at the same time and he found himself moaning instead. *"Mari."*

Marty's eyes rounded into the shape of full moons when it occurred to her that her bridal necklace was pulsing. Much like a Wani ring pulsed. Only a hundred times stronger...

"How. Fucking. Groovy."

Her eyes rolled back into her head as her mouth fell open dumbly.

Kil had but a second to grin before the climax hit him hard and he began to convulse and moan. *"Nee'ka,"* he growled as he came down on top of her and rode out wave after mind-numbing wave of orgasmic peak. *"Mari."*

Marty moaned and groaned as she rode out the waves with him, the euphoria of it close to maddening. She clutched his buttocks when he came down on top of her, her fingers digging into the steely flesh there.

She wanted him to consume her, to stay inside of her forever. When the peaks began to lessen and she was able once again to speak, she sighed contentedly and closed her eyes, not caring in the slightest that she'd just put on a show for every patron in the dining stall. "I love you, Kil," she murmured. "Forever."

Kil kissed her on the forehead, then raised his head to look at her. "I love—" He stopped when he realized that she was sound asleep.

The claiming. He'd forgotten that *nee'kas* often passed out soon after the claiming. Now that he thought on it he was surprised she'd managed to stay awake this long.

Grinning down into her face, he began to disentangle their bodies when an odd premonition passed over him. His smile faltering, the tiny hairs at the nape of his neck stirred when it dawned on him that his shaft was far more saturated than it should have been. Sitting up to withdraw from her fully, he felt as though he might be sick when he glanced down to where their bodies had been joined.

His stomach muscles clenched and knotted. Sweet juice. She was flooding sweet juice.

"Holy sands," Ora murmured as she and Jek came down beside him. Her features were shocked and horrified. "Mari is about to hatch, Mighty One."

Kil's hearts rate picked up to an alarming degree. "I just claimed her," he rasped out."

Ora closed her eyes briefly, her hand flying to her mouth to keep from crying out.

Jek shook his head slowly, then spoke the words all three of them knew to be true. "If she doesn't wake up to labor the *pani* sac..."

Kil's haunted eyes met his former bound servant's. They flicked toward Jek's. "They will both die," he murmured.

In the blink of an eye Kil summoned on his clothes and cradled his wife in his arms. Staggering toward the doors, he held her tightly as he got himself under control. He needed his wits about him. He needed to rein in his emotions.

"Please don't die," he said softly. "I love you, *nee'ka*..."

Kil's gut clenched and twisted when it occurred to him that for the second time in his life he was losing a woman he loved. And for the second time in his life, she was dying before he'd told her that he loved her.

Chapter Seventeen
Meanwhile, on the green moon of Ti Q'won...

ဢ

Jana's nostrils flared as she glanced toward her brother Dar. He was but one trading stall away. Too close. Too bedamned close.

"How in the name of the goddess will we ever pull this off?" Dari asked quietly, her glowing blue gaze flicking warily back and forth between her sister and cousin.

Kara's teeth sank down into her bottom lip. She nibbled on it for a second. "He's watching us too closely, Jana. 'Tis insanity to attempt —"

"Nay," Jana interrupted, her voice hushed. "'Twas a great deal of trouble to steal these two *qi'kas* away from the palace." She took a calming breath. "We must trade them for credits this day and well you know it."

Dari, the youngest of the princesses at fourteen Yessat years, was the least convinced. "I don't know, Jana. If Dar catches us he will tell *mani* and papa for a certainty." She shuddered. "Papa will be fierce angry that —"

"You would rather be given to Gio then?" Jana whispered. "For if you would then say so now and Kara and I will continue on without you."

Dari's eyes widened. "For a certainty I do not wish to be claimed on the moon-rising of my twenty-fifth birthday." She threw five or six long micro-braids over her shoulder. "Yet is Dar offering us no opportunity to be without his escort."

Kara picked up a bejeweled flask of perfume and feigned interest in it. "We have to figure out a way to distract him," she murmured, being careful to appear as though she was interested in their shopping. "Jana has the right of it, Dari. We must begin selling *qi'kas* at every opportunity so we've credits aplenty when the chance to escape arises."

Dari sighed, but nodded. "'Tis true, your words." She picked up a bicep bracelet and pretended to study it. "Tell me what to do and 'tis done."

Jana pondered that question for a suspended moment. "Create a diversion of sorts. Just long enough that I might slip into the next stall and arrange a trade."

"How long will you need?" Dari asked.

"Less than two Nuba-minutes," Kara supplied.

Dari took a deep breath, which thrust her young breasts out. She considered a few options but in the end only one felt as though it had a chance at working. "I'm going to openly flirt with the warriors here," she whispered.

Jana gasped. "Nay, sister, 'tis too much trouble you will bring down upon your head in the doing. You are still a girl-child, disallowed to dine with warriors let alone flirt with them." She shook her head. "Dar needs distracted, aye, but papa will bar you to your rooms or worse if you—"

"But it will work," Dari said with conviction. She was a modest girl, but also a practical one. She knew how strongly her dark skin and glowing blue eyes were coveted in Trek Mi Q'an, which meant it would be easy for her to find warriors to cause a diversion with. Girl-child or no, they would still flirt back. And Dar would be angered enough to be distracted. "If I flirt with the warriors here 'twill give the deuce of you time to make the trade." She paused for a moment and gazed at her sister and cousin without wavering. "I shall gladly suffer confinement to my rooms for a fortnight in exchange for my total freedom."

Kara squeezed her hand. "Are you certain you want to go through with this?"

"Aye."

"I admire your bravery, cousin."

Jana sighed. She didn't want her younger sister in trouble any more than Kara did, but like Kara she also realized that Dari's plan was liable to work. And more to the point, it was the only plan they had. "Okay then." She nodded, if a bit warily. "Distract away."

Glancing first over her shoulder to make certain none but her sister and cousin were watching, Dari quickly turned back to them and pinched at her own nipples until they stood stiffly under the top of her *kazi*. When she was certain they had plumped up in the way she'd often heard her sire and brothers say was desirable, she took a deep breath and began glancing around for unsuspecting warriors.

Dari's glowing blue gaze fell at last on an eight foot giant whose handsomeness fair took her young breath away. He was a High Lord or mayhap a warlord of a lesser title for he was growling out orders to the hunters in his employ. From what she could make out of their clipped conversation, 'twas apparent he and his entourage had ventured into Ti Q'won that he might trade credits for weaponry. All in Trek Mi Q'an knew, after all, that the Ti Q'woniis were highly skilled in the art of *zorg*-crafting.

Oh he was handsome for a certainty, Dari thought on a naïve sigh. Hair as black as the night, eyes that glowed a sensuous gold, and a gigantic muscular stature that made the warriors around him seem rather puny in comparison. Even the skull on his forehead was intriguing to Dari, for it gave him a sinister appeal that a sheltered young princess such as herself found wicked and untamed.

When Dari's young nipples plumped up further just looking at him, she knew he would be the one. Taking one last deep breath, she located her reserve of courage and began to walk towards him in slow strides.

Kara and Jana were so busy watching Dar that neither of them had taken notice of the warlord Dari was about to engage in conversation. If they had, both of them would have given her a fierce nay, for although Dari hadn't seen Lord Death in

years — since the days when he'd worn his hair shaved bald —
both of them had seen him recently. And both of them would
have known that by flirting with the very warlord who was
training Dari's betrothed in the warring arts, her brazen
escapades would reach Gio's ears for a certainty.

Chapter Eighteen

ಬಿ

"'Tis almost out, Mighty One."

From within the single bedchamber located aboard the King of Morak's high-speed conveyance, Ora sat behind Marty and propped up her limp, unconscious body. "I can scarce believe it," she whispered in awe-filled tones, "but 'tis working for a certainty."

Kil was unable to respond, for every cell of his being was fixated on his Sacred Mate's belly. He hadn't known it was possible either, but then again he hadn't known any warrior in all of his days who had found it necessary to mesmerize his own hatchling from its mother's womb.

It was painful — very painful. His entire body was damp with sweat, his face wet with tears. But he was determined. His hatchling would survive, and Jek would navigate the conveyance to Sand City and Ari before death befell his beloved *nee'ka*.

Kil could feel his tiny creation's terror, as if the unborn hatchling knew things were not as they were supposed to be. The wee one was not only afraid to leave the only home it had ever known, but its genetic imprint told it that its mother was not pushing, and therefore it was not time to enter this realm. But a stronger force kept pulling at it...

Kil gritted his teeth as he continued to coax the hatchling from its nest. Mesmerizing whilst telekinetically summoning was no easy feat and it was quickly zapping all of his strength. But he was almost there, just a wee bit more...

"'Tis coming!" Ora exclaimed.

Please Aparna, Kil silently prayed. *Please...*

"Just a bit more!"

Kil's jaw clenched. He could do this. Aye, he could do this.

"Almost," Ora said excitedly, which oddly gave Kil more strength. "Another few Nuba-seconds."

Kil's gaze brightened and simultaneously narrowed as he concentrated so intently he felt as though his head might split in two from the effort. *Come, wee one*, he coaxed. *Come to papa…*

"'Tis here!"

Exhausted, Kil still found enough strength to both laugh and cry as the *pani* sac slid into his hands. He could feel it pulsing, knew that the sac was alive and unharmed. His gaze shot up to Ora who was grinning from ear to ear.

"You did it!" she beamed, her hands clapping together. "Mari will be fierce proud of you when she wakes up and knows what you have done."

Kil's smile faltered as he glanced at his Sacred Mate—his very still and far too pale Sacred Mate. "How is she?" he rasped out.

"She is holding on," Ora declared with a crisp incline to her head. "She is very strong and she is holding on."

Kil nodded slowly, grateful to Ora for the physical and moral support she was providing. She had turned out to be a great help these past hours and for that reason alone he would see to it that she never wanted for anything. "You have my thanks," he said quietly, his energy greatly depleted.

Ora waved that away. "Mari is my dearest friend. I could do no less."

She cocked her head and smiled as she glanced down at the *pani* sac he was clutching. "What will you name the hatchling?"

He grinned, using one hand to wipe sweat from his brow. "I do not know yet."

But an hour later when the incubation period had ended and a tiny, feisty little warrior girl emerged, Kil knew exactly what he would name her. "Zy'an," he murmured, as he stroked the tuft of black hair atop her head. "I name you Zy'an."

Ora blinked back her tears. She knew as well as Kil did what the words *Zy'an* meant in the ancient tongue. And as she looked down into the newly hatched girl-child's visage, she had the oddest premonition that she had just witnessed the birth of a female who would grow up to be a woman very important to their people.

Zy'an.

The bringer of hope.

Chapter Nineteen
Meanwhile, on the green moon of Ti Q'won…

ဢ

"Please papa—no more!"

Dari cried out in pain and humiliation as her sire's hand came crashing down once again upon her naked buttocks. He was spanking her in the great hall for her entire family to witness, even her wee sister Hera. Bent over his knee, she could do naught but wait for her punishment to be finished.

Jana and Kara glanced toward each other warily, both of them feeling guilty.

"Dak please," Geris said worriedly as she strode closer, "I think she's learned her lesson."

Oh, Dari thought, she had learned her lesson for a certainty. She had learned to trust her sire as little as she trusted her betrothed. They were one in the same, cut from the same cloth. Both of them were uncaring for her feelings, both of them wanting naught but her obedience and the political alliance the future union would forge.

"She has shamed herself and my name!" Dak bellowed, his hand crashing down on Dari's buttocks again. "What think you Gio will say when he learns of this episode? And do not think for a moment, wife, that Death will not feel honor bound to inform him!"

Geris flinched when Dari cried out again. "Death was flattered by it," she stuttered out, wringing her hands together. "Dak please stop. I've never seen you like this!" She released a shaky breath. "You're scarin' me."

Dak's jaw clenched. "You mayhap have never seen me like this because I have never *felt* like this," he gritted out. He swatted her backside again, drawing more tears and pleading from Dari.

Kara's eyes narrowed at Dar since he was the bedamned warrior who had felt honor bound to confess Dari's actions to her sire. High Lord Death had been bemused by the princess' attention, flattered even, so she really didn't see what the big deal was about. No harm had been done.

To Dar's credit, he avoided Kara's gaze, looking a little uneasy himself. Clearly even he had not expected his sire to become this angry.

"Dak please!" Geris screeched, doing a little crying of her own. "You are really frightening me!"

Apparently having realized that his wife was serious, Dak immediately ceased his daughter's public spanking. He pulled the bottom of Dari's *kazi* down from her waist that it again covered her buttocks and let her up off of his knee.

The moment she was freed, Dari fled from the great hall in tears, sprinting toward her rooms as fast as her feet would carry her.

Kara and Jana exchanged another guilty glance. Dar shifted uneasily on his feet. Geris bit down onto her lip.

It was wee Hera who gave voice to what everyone was thinking. Popping her thumb out of her mouth, she said to her sire before walking away, "By the sands, papa, you are nigh unto a gulch beast this day."

* * * * *

"How do you feel?" Kara asked gently. She sat down next to Dari on her bed and began smoothing micro-braids back behind her ear. "Are you alright?"

Jana stood next to the raised bed nibbling on her bottom lip. She felt wickedly guilty. "'Tis sorry I am, sister. As the elder I never should have let you—"

"Nay," Dari said in a monotone voice, staring unblinking into space. "'Twas my decision and I harbor no regrets."

Kara's eyes widened. "Do you not?"

"Nay." Dari lay there unspeaking for a protracted silence, causing Jana and Kara to exchange worried glances. Finally, after long moments, Dari spoke, her voice devoid of all emotion. "I hate him," she whispered.

"Papa?" Jana asked anxiously.

"I hate him too," Dari said, wishing she did.

Kara took a deep breath. She knew Dari's anger toward her sire would pass, so she let that go. "'Tis Gio of whom you speak?"

"Aye." Dari propped herself up on her elbows and rested her chin in her palms. "'Twould not have been necessary to shame papa, nor to plot to run from mine own home, did he not persist in his desire to claim me against my will."

Kara sighed as she stroked her back, knowing precisely how her cousin felt.

Jana's gaze flicked back and forth between her sister and cousin. "I pray that the deuce of you realize the consequences of our escape, if 'tis indeed successful."

Kara and Dari both turned their heads to look at her.

Jana smiled sadly. "We will never see our families again," she said softly. She thought of her *mani* and papa, of her siblings—even bedamned Dar, and suppressed the need to cry. "We can never come back…not ever."

All three girls were quiet for a moment as they each thought about the families that they would be leaving behind. But in the end all three agreed that 'twas better to leave and miss them than to stay only that their sires might give them away to warlords not of their choosing. Either way they would be removed from their birth homes the soonest.

"'Tis settled then," Jana announced, if a bit sadly. "The three of us shall flee together that we might choose our own destinies."

Kara and Dari nodded. "'Tis a vow," they whispered simultaneously.

Silence fell once again within the bedchamber until Dari broke the silence. "Was today's quest successful?" she asked. "Or was my punishment in vain?"

"Nay," Kara assured her. "'Twas successful for a certainty."

Dari looked at her as if wanting details. It was Jana, however, who provided them.

"We were successful beyond our wildest expectations," she said with rounded eyes. Jana tossed a long golden tress over her shoulder. "Neither Kara nor I had any idea royal *qi'kas* would fetch such large sums."

Kara took a deep breath. "One hundred thousand credits a piece," she murmured. "I can still scarce believe it."

Dari's jaw dropped open. "Surely you jest."

"Nay." Jana shook her head. "We've the money to go."

Dari nodded. "So all we have left to do is figure out how to escape."

Kara squeezed her hand. "Aye," she murmured.

Chapter Twenty
The Palace of the Dunes, Sand City on Planet Tryston

જી

With his unconscious *nee'ka* cradled in his arms, Kil sprinted at top speed from the conveyance launching pad. Upon reaching the great hall, he realized that Ari must have been expecting them for as soon as the Chief Priestess laid eyes upon them, Mari's still form dissolved from his arms with Ari disappearing a blink of an eye behind her.

"Where did she take her?" Kil bellowed to Zor, who was rushing up to his side. It was apparent that he too knew what was happening. Ari, in all if her inexplicable wisdom, must have somehow foreseen his coming.

"To the apartments you keep here," Zor informed him, his eyes searching Kil's face worriedly. "Ari asks that you leave her be to work on your *nee'ka*. She will inform you when 'tis safe to disturb her."

Kil sighed, raking punishing hands through his hair. Ignoring his brother, he turned about in a semi-circle to see if Ora was behind him. When he saw her and the baby safely in her arms, he motioned her over, needing to hold his wee daughter.

Zy'an cooed the moment he plucked her from Ora's arms, her motor skills already evolving at a rapid rate these past few hours. He kissed her atop her fluffy head, running his nose through the silky stuff, loving her baby scent.

Kil turned back to Zor who was busy grinning down at his wee niece. "'Tis worried I am," Kil said hoarsely. "I managed to birth her, yet has she not eaten. She refused the *taka* juice, spitting it up all over me."

Zor thought that over for a moment. He held out his arms for the babe that he might hold her. "Mayhap she will drink of the *mali* juice."

"Nay." Kil shook his head, his worry apparent. "I tried that as well. She isn't able to keep down any of it."

Just then Kyra came into the great hall with her youngest son Jun holding her hand. She walked quickly towards the brothers, wanting to find out what was going on.

Zor and Kil looked at Kyra's engorged breasts and then at each other. They both blew out a breath at the same time, having simultaneously realized that 'twas possible Zy'an might take to another *mani's* sweet juice.

"Oh my god," Kyra panted as she finally reached them. "Zora and Zara just told me what happened." She glanced worriedly down at the baby. "How is she?"

"She could be better," Kil rasped out, running a finger gently down his daughter's cheek.

"Can I do anything to help?" Kyra asked, her eyes rounded.

Zor quickly brought her up to speed. Kyra immediately took Zy'an from her husband's arms and settled down with her at the raised table in the dining hall.

Twenty Nuba-minutes later, Kil blew out a breath of relief. Zy'an had accepted her Auntie's offering. She had even smiled after she'd belched.

* * * * *

Much later that moon-rising, Kil was at last escorted into the bedchamber where Mari lay. Her eyes were still closed, she was still unconscious, and from what Ari had told him, she was yet to wake up. The only solace Kil had was that her color had restored somewhat.

"Do not give up hope," Ari murmured. "Her will is strong. Just keep telling her how much you and Zy'an need her, how important it is for her to keep from crossing through the *Rah*."

Kil nodded, understanding that the *Rah* was the unnatural barrier lying between this realm and the mystical world of the goddess. He held Zy'an securely as he settled down next to Mari on the raised bed.

His eyes flicked over his *nee'ka's* form, noting at once that she was naked and that her sweet juice had already come in. He blew out a breath, telling himself that surely 'twas a good sign.

When Ari's form shimmered and dissolved, Kil turned to his wife and took her still hand in his.

"Please," he said hoarsely, his words thick with emotion, "come back to us, Mari." A single tear tracked down his cheek. "I love you, *nee'ka*. I love you with all of my hearts."

No response.

Kil sighed wearily, but refused to give up hope. So long as she breathed, there was always hope. "Come back to me, little one."

Chapter Twenty-One

ဢ

"I love you nee'ka. I love you with all of my hearts."

Pain. So much pain. Marty tried to return to the voice, but it hurt so much. She loved the voice, needed the voice, but the pain of reaching it made her cry out.

"Come back to me, little one."

She wanted to come back. She ached to come back. She tried once more but—the pain. The pain was unbearable.

Marty floated away from the voice. It occurred to her that the further away she went from the voice, the less pain she felt.

So peaceful. So painless and peaceful.

Marty floated further and further away until at last the pain was gone. When she got far enough away she was able to see again. Shimmering gold. Lots of gold. An entrance.

Q'i Liko Aki Jiq—She Who Is Borne of the Goddess.

Marty surpassed the entrance and floated inside.

Naked priestesses. Chanting. They meant to keep her out, keep her from peace, keep her from the Rah.

No.

Marty continued floating up to them. She had only to breach their energy wall and the beautiful peace would be hers. So close. Just a bit further…

But they sensed her, damn them. She had tried to keep quiet, but they sensed her presence any way.

The priestesses grew frightened and called out to her, to the strongest amongst their kind. And then she was there. The most powerful mortal in existence. Naked and chanting.

Trying to keep Marty from bypassing her energy to breach the Rah.

The powerful one was sweating. She was in pain. She closed her eyes and Marty knew that she had her. She was strong, yes, but Marty's need to feel no pain was stronger.

Marty floated up to the powerful one's energy and began to attack it. The Chief Priestess cried out, but held strong. She would not be easy, but Marty knew her will was stronger.

Marty backed up then attacked the mystical field full force. The powerful one cried out in pain, stumbled a bit. In that moment Marty knew that the Chief Priestess' energy was depleting.

She gathered together all of her strength, all of her mite, and prepared to breach the powerful one's energy once and for all with one last tactical maneuver. But...

"Please nee'ka. I love you. Zy'an loves you. We need you."

The voice. The voice was in pain. The voice was looking upon her former body and knew that she was going to the Rah.

She wanted the voice to stop her. Yes! Yes! She needed the voice. She needed the voice more than anything. She began to float back towards it—

Sharp pain. Splintering pain—Agony.

Marty turned away from the voice, away from the pain, and determined to breach the Rah. She faced off with the powerful one again, determined to knock past her barricades.

The voice had given the powerful one time to regroup, but her energy was still depleting. Marty went in for the kill, determined to breach the Rah once and for all. She began floating towards the Rah at top speed. She would breach it. She would—

The powerful one cried out as she used all of her energy to throw up one last barricade. A dreamscape. She had erected a dreamscape allowing but one from the goddess' realm to breach the Rah and come to this side.

For the first time, Marty felt afraid. The dreamscape opened to reveal a woman of golden hair and glowing blue eyes—a woman whose will was stronger than her own.

Jana. The mother of the voice.

The golden woman stood before the Rah, defiantly challenging Marty to dare cross her to breach it. Marty accepted the gauntlet she threw down and flew at her full force. The impact of hitting her sent Marty reeling backwards, sharp pain splintering through her. She cried out, for the first time hearing her own voice.

The sentinel was even more powerful than the one who had let her through to this side. But Marty tried again, flying at her with everything she had, determined to win and breach the Rah. The next impact made her cry out again.

Pain—even worse than the pain it took to reach the voice.

"I love you, nee'ka."

The voice was calling out to her again.

Marty fled from the sentinel, back to the voice. The voice would protect her. The voice would never let her feel pain again. She had but to breach the barrier that separated her from the voice and the voice would make the pain go away.

Marty screamed as she flew at top speed towards the mortal barrier, determined to break through it once and for all. If only she could reach the voice. One more attack and she would breach—

Marty gasped and cried out as she re-entered her body.

It was painful, so painful, but she knew she had done it.

She glanced back at the sentinel one last time and smiled in thanks. The sentinel inclined her head in return, her glowing blue eyes filled with happiness.

Proudly, Jana turned back and re-entered the dreamscape, disappearing as she breached the Rah.

Chapter Twenty-Two
Crystal City on the planet Galis
One week later

෨

Kari Gy'at Li, once known as Kara Marie Summers, felt her nipples harden of their own volition as she glanced down from the stage she was performing on and into the glowing gold gaze of the largest, fiercest-looking warrior she'd come into contact with in all of the years she'd been in this dimension.

He was a giant, a veritable gargantuan. The very kind of territorial alpha male her adoptive sisters had warned her off from.

But the way he was studying her, the way that his brooding eyes flicked over every square inch of her body and coveted it...it was more arousing than words could describe.

Kari boldly met the warlord's golden gaze as she sat down before him on the stage and spread her thighs wide apart. His eyes immediately flew to the flesh between her legs and she could hear his breathing grow shallow as he gazed there.

Kari felt desire knot in her belly as she wickedly ran her fingers through the thatch of wine-red hair covering her mons. The giant's eyes tracked the movement, seeing everything, missing nothing.

Her pink nipples plumped up, hardening and elongating from the puffy pads that were her areolas. Watching him watch her was the most arousing thing she'd ever experienced.

Kari began to play with herself in the way she knew that the visiting warriors liked, massaging her labia and clit in slow, teasing circles. She could feel herself getting wetter and wetter, could feel her dew saturating her fingers as she continued to tantalize the warlord with her enticing finger-play.

The warlord, paying no heed whatsoever to protocol, reached over and began massaging her breasts, his large hands palming them, then plucking at the nipples while Kari stroked her pussy for his viewing enjoyment.

She shivered as her nipples hardened impossibly further. She offered the giant no resistance when his mouth latched onto one with a groan and suctioned it into the heat of his mouth. Kari released a shaky breath as he sucked on her. She arched her back so that her breasts thrust out and pressed further against his face.

The warlord released her nipple, leaving a popping sound in its wake, then used both hands to draw her pearly white breasts together as close as they would go. He grunted with satisfaction when he managed to make the nipples stand side by side, then lowered his face to her chest and suctioned both nipples into his mouth at the same time.

Kari gasped, the hand that had been toying with her clit falling limply to her side. She moaned as he lapped at her ripe nipples, then groaned as he suckled vigorously on them like lollipops.

She sat there on the stage for the longest time, knowing that the dining stall was packed and that all eyes were greedily devouring her, and allowed the warlord to break the rules, to suck and suck on her nipples to his hearts' content.

But it seemed that he'd never get his fill. Five minutes ticked by. Then ten. Then fifteen. And still the giant sucked on her nipples, his eyes closed in bliss as he sipped from her ripe peaks over and over, again and again.

Kari wanted more. She was so hot, so aroused, that she knew she'd allow this gigantic warrior to do anything he wanted to her. And she wanted him to do anything—to do everything. She'd heard all the stories, knew that women meant nothing to warriors other than giving them bodies to play with like toys, yet in that moment she wanted to be the toy that he played with more than she wanted to breathe.

Falling slowly onto her back, Kari closed her eyes and released a shaky breath as she felt her shoulders hit the soft stage. The giant ceased his suckling and she could feel his aroused gaze on her, waiting to see if she would offer herself to him.

Without even opening her eyes, she spread her thighs as wide as they would go, telling him without words that she wanted him to mount her. Right there on the stage for everyone to see. She was in heat for him and she wanted him to ride her.

Death's glowing gold eyes narrowed in desire as he studied every nuance of the wench's body. Her eyes were closed, her nipples were stabbing upward, and the pelt of fire-berry hair covering her mons was glistening from her own dew.

He had never wanted a wench more.

The scent of her arousal intoxicated him, made his staff hard as an ice-jewel. But before he mounted her, he needed to taste her.

Sliding her hips to the end of the stage, Death's tongue shot out to taste her, making one long lick from the opening of her channel, up between her labial lips, not stopping until he reached the clit. The wench moaned, making his staff impossibly harder.

Death drew the tiny erect clit into his mouth and suckled on it as vigorously as he had her nipples. The wench's body convulsed as she groaned, shaking all around him as he lapped at her like a starved animal.

He made her come four times—four euphoric, delirious times during which the erotic arts apprentice transferred her bliss to the audience and made all of them—himself included—spurt four violent, wicked times.

And yet still he craved her sweet pussy, still he wanted to taste it and play with it, still he wanted to lap at the juice it provided him with, to lave it with his tongue and latch onto its little clit that he might suckle of it.

Death kept his face buried between her thighs for the better part of an hour, wringing orgasm after orgasm after orgasm out of the gasping, pleading, writhing, begging wench, who kept screaming at him to fuck her and fill up her cunt with his cum.

"Please," she screamed out, her nipples stabbed permanently skyward, her body convulsing from yet another orgasm, *"please fuck me."*

Death could have happily lapped at her pussy for another hour or so, yet the wench's pleading was becoming hysterical. She was nigh unto sobbing, so desirous of a hard ride she was.

Summoning off his leather garb, he slid the wench's hips all the way down the stage and stood between them. Grabbing a thigh in either hand, he guided the tip of his cock to her saturated channel and, with one possessive thrust, slid into her wet flesh to the hilt.

"Oh yes," she screamed, her hips arching for a deep, hard ride, *"oh yes."*

"Mmm," Death rumbled out, his voice a rough purr. His fingers played in her thatch of fire-berry hair. "'Tis made for my fucking, this channel." He stroked into her to the hilt, causing her to instantly orgasm.

"More," she begged. "I need more."

"Beg me again," he rumbled out arrogantly, his strokes still slow and leisurely. "Beg me to do anything of my desire to you and your sweet channel."

Kari threw her hips at him wildly, at that moment more than willing to say anything if it meant he'd cease tormenting her and give her the hard pounding she needed. "You can do anything you want to me," she sobbed. "My body belongs to you." She didn't know enough about warriors to realize she'd just made a vow to him.

Arrogantly satisfied that he'd gotten the oath he'd sought, that he would not have to satisfy himself with one fuck, Death gave her exactly what she wanted, pounding into her flesh with deep, hard, quick strokes.

Kari came again—harder this time—causing the audience and her gigantic tormenter to moan and groan.

He reached underneath her, palmed her buttocks, and sank into her with quicker, deeper strokes. "Mine," he said hoarsely. "'Tis my channel now."

She threw her hips at him wildly, groaning when he leaned over to lick her nipples as he burrowed deeper and deeper into her flesh. *"Harder,"* she begged him, not caring at the moment how submissive she sounded. *"Fuck me harder."*

He ground his hips at her, then pounded away mercilessly into her flesh. His tongue flicked at her hard nipples, sipping them in to draw from while he gave her a hard ride.

Kari moaned, her hips thrashing about violently. *"I'm coming,"* she groaned. *"Oh god I'm coming."*

Death picked up the pace of his thrusting, sinking into her wet flesh faster and faster, deeper and harder. His fingers dug into her buttocks. "Now," he commanded her. "Come for me *now.*"

She obeyed him on a moan, her nipples jutting up to the point of pain, her face heating to the point of breaking into a sweat, as she closed her eyes and violently came all over his shaft.

Transference occurred once again, only Death felt the tremors much harsher than the audience. For the first time in his life, he bellowed loud enough to wake the dead as he spurted deep inside of her lusty channel.

Exhausted, he fell on top of her and licked her nipples.

Kari smiled as she fell asleep right there on the stage, her fingers running through the warlord's thick black hair.

He thought her nipples were his personal lollipops. She loved it.

Chapter Twenty-Three
Sand City on planet Tryston

80

"Let's recap my life since having met you, shall we?"

Kil grunted at his beloved and very much recovered *heeka-beast* of a wife. "Except for almost dying," he sniffed, "it has been nigh unto bliss for a certainty."

Marty rolled her eyes. "Oh yeah, it's been real groovy." Her lips puckered into a frown. "Especially the bit about being thrown into a harem and forced into sexual slavery. Yeah, I can see why other warriors might come to you for hot dating tips."

"Mari," he warned with a growl.

"You should write a handbook on the subject," she said grandly. *"Wench Wooing 101: How To Get Women To Flee From You In Terror."*

His jaw clenched. "Must you keep bringing this up? For days my brothers have been making jest of me." He groaned. "I have heard every bedamned joke in the galaxies. How many dunces does it take to recognize a Sacred Mate?" he mimicked with a roll of his eyes. He went on to list a few more of his brothers' favorite ribbings. "Must you, my own *nee'ka*, make sport of me as well?"

Marty didn't so much as hesitate in her answer. "Yes."

He grunted. "Now that you are recovered, mayhap a swat to your backside is in order."

"Let me guess..." Marty squinted her eyes shut and dramatically clapped a hand to her forehead. "Oh yeah," she said as she opened her eyes, "that bit of hot wooing advice

comes from Chapter three in your handbook: *Wives &
Children — What's the Big Dif?*"

"Well," he growled, "I see that you are ready to return to
your nest in Koror."

Marty grinned. "You're such a big baby," she teased.
"Lighten up."

Kil gathered her closer in his arms where they laid
together on the bed. His hands ran over her engorged breasts,
stopping to plump up the nipples. "Tell me you love me," he
purred.

She laid her head on his chest and sighed contentedly. "I
love you, Kil Q'an Tal. With all of my heart."

He harrumphed. "With only one heart?"

"I only have one heart."

"Oh, aye," he mumbled. He ran one large palm down her
backside and kneaded a buttock. "I love you with two hearts."

Marty smiled as she ran a hand over his chest. Ever since
she'd woken up from having almost died Kil couldn't seem to
stop telling her how much he loved her. Not that she was
complaining. "I know you do. But thanks for saying it out
loud."

He grunted. Marty smiled.

"I'm curious about something," she said, changing the
subject.

"Aye?"

"Giselle…" Her brow wrinkled. "I really like her a lot and
all, but why — uh…" She cleared her throat. "How come every
time you turn around she's popping her nipple into your
brother's mouth?"

Kil chuckled. "Because she is a good and submissive
nee'ka. Mayhap you could take lessons from her."

Marty snorted at that.

He grinned. "I am but teasing you." He went on to
explain what had become of Rem from his years with Jera and

how, even though he was progressing in leaps and bounds, he was still recovering from his devolution.

"No kidding. And the nipple thing really helps?"

"Aye. 'Tis the only remedy Giselle has found thus far that actually works."

Marty shook her head and sighed. "Somehow I'm not surprised."

Kil groaned as he rolled Marty onto her back and latched his mouth around one of her swollen nipples. He closed his eyes in bliss as he sipped from it, causing Marty to sigh contentedly. After long minutes, he raised his head from her breasts, panting.

"'Tis no surprise to me either," he said thickly, rubbing his erection against her.

"Huh?" Marty gulped, having lost the thread of the conversation. It felt like forever since she and Kil had been together. And, of course, the requisite two week waiting period in between giving birth and resuming sexual relations meant forever would last a little longer. Three days to be precise.

He chuckled. "Never mind." The sound of Zy'an crying drew his attention to the other side of the bedchamber.

"She's probably hungry," Marty said with a laugh.

Kil grinned back. Their daughter's voracious appetite had become somewhat of a running joke between them. Actually it had become a running joke amongst the entire Q'an Tal family, for Zy'an loved to eat with the same zealousness that warriors liked to make love.

Marty smiled as her eyes flicked toward her baby's crystal cradle. *Her baby*—she couldn't get over it. When she'd fallen into that coma-like state she hadn't even known she was pregnant! But when she'd woken up, she'd found out that she had given birth to the most beautiful black haired, glowing blue eyed little girl that had ever lived. Of course, she was admittedly biased. "I better go feed Princess Greedy."

"Nay." Kil sat up. "Prop yourself up on the pillows. I will get my daughter."

Marty's heart never failed to flutter whenever she saw father and daughter together. Kil was so huge and gruff, riddled with battle scars and not prone toward smiling. Yet whenever Zy'an was in his arms, he couldn't seem to stop smiling. Or cooing—a fact she found adorable.

Marty smiled as she watched her naked husband pad over to the baby's cradle. God he was sexy, she thought. His entire body rippled of muscle when he walked. And that butt—yummy. She still had a hard time believing she had managed to make the warlord all hers. But she had.

She had set out to gain all or nothing. And she had finally gotten it all.

Definitely groovy.

* * * * *

"Bloody hell," Giselle muttered, "I don't know about this."

Marty glanced from where Rem was standing on the other side of the great hall chatting with his brothers back to Giselle who was sitting next to her. "You think it's too soon?"

She sighed. "The Chief Priestess said he was supposed to steer clear of Consummation Feasts for years. Your feast is scheduled in two days time. Yes, I think it's too soon."

Kyra patted her on the hand. "After giving the subject more thought, Ari changed her mind. She thinks this is just what Rem needs." She shrugged. "The sooner his life becomes everything normal, everything it would have been if Jera hadn't interfered, then the sooner the demons will be laid to rest as it were."

Marty snorted. "And to think that to our husbands a Consummation Feast *is* normal." She sighed. "All I can say after having lived with Kil for the amount of time I have is that I am not surprised."

Giselle's lips puckered into a frown as she bounced her son Kilak on her knee. Her daughter Zari was currently being shown off by Rem. "I'm not certain if it's Rem or me who's going to have the hardest time adjusting to this. Call me old fashioned or hopelessly earthy, but the idea of bound servants sucking my husband off whilst I watch hardly inspires me to want to show up to this little soiree."

Kyra chuckled. "Make sure you sit next to Geris then. After all of these years she still throws a fit at the precise moment Dak comes." She grinned. "Of course, she always gets back at him when it's the women's turn."

Marty harrumphed. "I, for one, am looking forward to it." Her fingers tapped absently on the raised table. "Having spent time in a certain dunce's harem, I can't wait to piss him off by letting other warriors touch me." She recalled how possessively he'd made love to her after Death had fondled her in the dining hall that time. "And Kyra's right, Gis, the sex will be soooo hot afterwards."

Giselle found herself grinning. "Promise?"

Kyra and Marty glanced at each other, then back to Giselle. "Oh yeah," they said in unison.

Chapter Twenty-Four
Meanwhile, on the planet of Galis…

ꙮ

"Show these people your submissiveness to me, Kari. Show them your desire to please me in all things."

Kari felt her nipples plumping up from the mere rumble of his dark voice. She was like Pavlov's dog, she thought. She'd do anything to keep fucking him. She was addicted to him and his cock and they both knew it.

"Alright," she whispered.

Naked, Kari threaded her hand through the giant's and allowed him to lead her down the crystal staircase of her suite, which led to the eating establishment she worked at below. Once there they didn't stop, but continued on outside and walked hand-in-hand down the busy white crystal street.

Galians were everywhere and they stared. At her, at him—at them. She was, after all, completely naked. And he was, after all, fully clothed.

On Galis, that didn't happen. On Galis, women ruled men sexually and otherwise, not the other way around. But the warlord who had been mounting Kari day and night in her suite for the past straight week was as possessive and domineering as he was addicting. He wanted her to publicly announce to the Galians of Crystal City who it was that her pussy belonged to, who it was that had been riding her hard all of this time.

Kari knew that if this episode got back to her adoptive family she would never hear the end of it. And truly, Kari knew that she was going to have to leave Crystal City to get away from him—and soon. Before she got any more addicted, before she wasn't able to leave him at all. But until then…

Death released her hand to lay his heavily muscled arm across her shoulder. He clamped it around her possessively, territorially, publicly marking her as his. His large hand began rubbing her breasts, massaging them in the way he knew made her hot for him. And then his thumb and forefinger found a nipple and plucked at it, rolling it around to harden and elongate it.

There were curious eyes everywhere. They followed the giant and the naked flame-haired woman as they walked down the street. They watched as the warlord played with her breasts, with her nipples, and then down lower...

Kari released a shaky breath when his hand left her breasts and trailed down over her tummy, then down lower still. His fingers sifted through her pubic hair as if petting her. He made no move to go lower, for he was arrogantly content to pet her there for all to see, showing the Galians that he had the right to do it.

He was definitely all warrior, Kari thought. Arrogant and domineering, possessive and commanding. He was everything her adoptive sisters had warned her to stay away from, everything that they'd said would be her downfall if she allowed one to mesmerize her.

Granted, her sisters didn't know a lot about warriors, for Galians tended to deliberately steer clear of them except when performing the erotic arts. But at all other times it was considered taboo to let one touch you. There were legends, after all. Legends about strange necklaces being clasped about female necks, only to have those very females be taken away and...well none of the Galians were quite certain what happened to the females after that. But Galian women had their guesses, and all of those guesses were grim.

Kari glanced up uneasily at the warlord beside her, noting that he wore one of those strange necklaces himself. What if he took it off? What if he clasped it about her neck and she was never heard heads or tales from again? What would he do with her then?

She gulped a little roughly, a thousand dismal scenarios running through her mind. She had already let Death — good lord his name was Death! — and she had already let him do things to her body that no man had ever done.

No, she had done more than *let* him. She had begged him, at times even sobbed for him to do it. He knew how to work a dark magic on her body that left her feeling as though she had no free will anymore, as though she would do anything and say anything for just one more intoxicating taste of his skill.

It had only been a week — one gloriously carnal week — and already he had taken her in every way there was for a man to take a woman. In the mouth, in the ass, sliding between her oiled up breasts, sinking into her pussy more times than she could count. He had tied her up then licked and fucked her mindless. He had taken her on all fours. He had commanded her to ride him. He had finger-fucked her, tongue-fucked her, even toe-fucked her. He had taken her in every way imaginable and unimaginable.

Kari shivered as she walked beside him, allowing him to show her off like an exotic, submissive doll. She had to leave him, she knew. It was past time to leave him. Because as all-consuming as the sex was, it was the warlord himself she felt addicted to, and that simply would not do.

It was strange, but there were times when she felt an inexplicable connection to him, as though she was able to gage his emotions. She knew that his emotions were powerful — very territorial, very alpha, very willing to kill any male who should touch her.

And he would. She knew that he would. From the moment he'd first sank his cock into her up on that stage a week ago, she had belonged to him in his eyes.

But belonged to him as what? A mistress? A toy? A...what?

"Take me into your mouth, little one."

161

Kari's head shot up to look at him. She'd been so preoccupied with her thoughts that she hadn't even realized they had stopped walking.

Her gaze darted about warily. They were standing in the middle of one of the busiest streets in Crystal City. People were watching them, staring at them. And he wanted her to publicly suck him off. On a planet where men gave pleasure to women, he wanted her to give pleasure to him for all eyes to see.

"Take me into your mouth," he murmured.

She could see the huge erection bulging against his dark blue leather pants. She could feel the gazes of passersby watching to see what she would do as he removed his cock from his pants and it sprang loose, hard and wanting her attention. In the end her addiction would allow her to do but one thing.

Kari sucked him off right there in the middle of Crystal City, not giving a damn who saw her do it. She sucked on him and sucked on him, the sound of her lips suctioning his cock into her mouth there for anyone to hear it.

When he came, it was violent, and his bellow of arrogant warrior satisfaction could be heard a long ways off. He spurted hot cum into her mouth and she greedily drank of it, wanting more and more and more and more of the sweet liquid.

She knew she had pleased him when he patted her on the head and murmured "good girl". She didn't bothering responding, though, because she was too busy suckling his balls to get him hard again.

Chapter Twenty-Five
Sand City, Two Days Later

෨

Oh yeah. She was jealous.

Marty hadn't expected to feel this way, not after her time in the harem when she'd seen him fondle other women and hadn't had the comfort of knowing that he loved her to fall back on, but oddly, now that she was his wife, the jealousy was there. Kinda stupid considering the fact that she had watched him do everything to Ora short of sinking his penis into her.

That night when she, Kil, and Ora had taken part in a threesome of sorts, Marty had felt turned on watching him suck Ora's nipples, watching him eat Ora out while she moaned, writhed, and came. She wasn't certain what the difference was between then and now, but she suspected it was because she trusted Ora where she didn't trust these other women. She knew what went on in the minds of the bound servants because she'd been one.

Seated next to her on the women's side of the great hall, Ora ran a hand over Marty's engorged breasts as she watched Kil slither his tongue about the labial folds of a busty bound servant. "Hers can't compare to these," she murmured in Marty's ear.

Marty grinned as she opened her legs so Ora could massage her intimately. Her and Ora's relationship was a tad strange for earth standards, she conceded, but considered normal for Trystonni ones. She and Ora loved each other— they were best friends—but they were not *in* love. And yet they harbored a strong sexual attraction towards one another that sometimes culminated in erotic touching.

"You know," Ora said as she played with Marty's pussy, "I have never been to a royal Consummation Feast before. Leastways not on this side of things." She chuckled. "I am looking forward to this."

"Me too."

Marty's eyes narrowed as she tracked the scene across the great hall. Two bound servants were sucking her husband off while he lapped at the pussy of a third.

The bound servant was gasping and moaning from where she sat perched on a raised table, her thighs spread as wide as they could go, her hands pressing Kil's face into her flesh. "Oh aye," the servant moaned, her nipples jutting out while he licked her, *"oh aye."*

Marty's nostrils flared.

—Arrg!

"Mmmm," Kil purred in that seductive growl of his. He flicked his tongue in rapid movements against her clit for a few seconds, then took the sensitive piece of flesh between his lips and suckled it hard until she screamed and came. A moment later he was bursting into the mouths of the bound servants sucking him off, groaning loudly as he climaxed.

"'Twas excellent," he praised them, patting both bound servants on the head. He fingered the vagina of the bound servant he had been licking. "And 'twas a fair tempting repast you offered unto me." He turned his head and grinned at Zor. "Shall we trade, brother?"

Marty was distracted from the scene across the great hall when Giselle growled from beside her. "I'm going to kill him," she fumed. "Rem is a dead man."

Marty glanced toward where Giselle's husband was seated next to Dak. Yep, she couldn't blame her. Rem was spewing into a bound servant's mouth, his lips latched around yet another one's nipple while he groaned.

"We'll get our turn," she assured Giselle. Her teeth gritted when she looked back at Kil. "Definitely."

"We bloody well better..." Giselle's voice trailed off when she turned her head to look at Marty. She sighed in resignation when she realized what it was Ora's hand was doing to Marty's vagina. "Et tu Brute?"

Marty's brow winkled. "Huh?"

"Never mind." Giselle waved dismissively. "I forgot you herald from the sixties. Make love, not war, etcetera, etcetera." She sighed dramatically.

Marty and Ora chuckled. "Hey I've been in this dimension longer than you, Gis." Marty grinned. "Give it a month and you might be surprised at the things you'll find yourself doing."

Giselle blushed. "I admit that I have fun at my baths — " Her teeth clicked shut when a giggling bound servant pressed Rem's face in between her legs. "I'll kill him," she seethed. "He's dead."

"Bastard!"

All eyes flew to Geris as she bolted to her feet and screamed out her war cry. Kyra grinned from where she sat next to her, having come to view Geris' reaction to Dak's orgasm as an ingrained ritual no Consummation Feast should be without.

"'Tis naught but tradition, my hearts." Dak groaned out the words as he came into a bound servant's mouth.

"Jek!" Geris wailed as her hands balled into fists. "It's time for the women. Come over here and service me!"

Jek grinned as he bowed, then took three long strides and snatched the Queen of Ti Q'won up into his arms. "Your pleasure is mine."

"Make me come really hard," Geris fumed as Jek laid her down on a *vesha* pad. Her nostrils flared. "Make me scream."

"Don't I always, my beauty?" Jek said as his face disappeared between her legs.

Giselle giggled as she watched. Then she gasped when she was picked up into a warrior's strong arms. She swallowed a bit nervously when she saw who it was. Gio. Her own niece's betrothed. "Oh dear."

"Do you not desire to make your Sacred Mate green with jealousy?" he murmured. His gaze flicked over her face, down lower to her breasts, then lower still.

Good lord, she thought, he was powerfully handsome. And the way his glowing violet eyes devoured a woman…very sexy indeed. She couldn't begin to imagine why Dari didn't want heads or tails to do with him. "Yes," she heard herself say unequivocally. Her bridal necklace began to pulse a warning red-green. "Definitely," she seethed.

Gio's grim masculine features lightened a bit when he grinned. "Good," he said, "for I'm of a mind to lick every spot on your body."

"Bloody hell," Giselle squeaked.

Marty was so busy laughing at Geris and Giselle that she hadn't realized Ora had left to find pleasure with Cam and Var, or that Death was standing beside her, his golden gaze heatedly flicking over her.

"It occurs to me," Death murmured, "that I never did get to taste of you."

Startled, Marty's gaze flew up to meet the grim giant's. She licked her lips, remembering how aroused he had made her when he'd sucked her nipples. "You forgot about me the moment Typpa started sucking you off," she teased him good-naturedly.

His lips curled into a semi-smile as he plucked Marty off of her chair. "Nay. But I sensed from Kil's reaction that something was amiss, so I let it be."

She wound her arms around his neck and grinned. "Thanks for salvaging my ego. You weren't supposed to give me up that easily, you know. That hadn't been a part of my grand plan."

Death found himself grinning—an unusual state of affairs for him—as he lowered Marty to a *vesha* pad. "I knew what you were about," he rumbled as he plucked her *qi'ka* top from her engorged breasts. His eyes narrowed in desire as he lowered his head and ran a tongue across one swollen nipple. "And I vow to make him more jealous this moon-rising than I did the last time."

Marty grinned as her breathing hitched. She spread her thighs so Death could settle his large form between them. "I always knew I liked you," she breathed out. And indeed he had been right. Her bridal necklace was all but smoking, letting her know without glancing his way that Kil was mightily pissed.

Groovy.

Death smiled against her breasts but said nothing. Drawing an elongated nipple into his mouth, he sucked on it thoroughly, slowly working his lips up and down it from tip to root, over and over again.

"Oh," Marty sighed, closing her eyes, "that feels so groovy."

His tongue flicked at her blue nipple ring.

"Very groovy," she groaned.

Death chuckled as his hands made the skirt of her *qi'ka* melt away. He kissed a path from her breasts to her belly, then down lower, his lips and nose running through the honey-gold curls on her mons.

"Yes," Marty panted as she spread her thighs as wide as they could go. "Please."

He toyed with her, running his tongue about her labial folds, sucking on the lips, getting oh so close to her clit, but not quite touching it.

"Please," she moaned as her hips arched up for him, *"please."*

Death buried his face between her legs with a groan, lapping at her flesh with mind-numbing strokes. His mouth latched around her clit and vigorously sipped from it, wringing groan after groan from the woman pinned beneath him.

Marty gasped as he drew harder from the clit, then groaned when she felt two more mouths latch onto her nipples and suckle. She glanced down at her breasts to see that Jek and Cam were feasting on her, drinking from her, both of them apparently having already made Geris and Ora climax.

She was the guest of honor, Marty remembered. She was the one who would be sucked and licked until she was sobbing from a violent climax.

Cam's tongue found her nipple ring and flicked at it rapidly.

Marty moaned.

Jek's mouth latched around her other nipple and sipped from her while his fingers found her navel ring and flicked it.

Marty groaned.

Death drew harder from her clit, suckling it vigorously while his throat emitted guttural sounds of primal male arousal.

Marty burst.

"Oh god," she screamed as her body shook and convulsed. *"Oh my god."*

She was given no time to come down from her high. One second three warriors had been laving at her with fingers and tongues and a blink of an eye later one possessive and majorly worked up alpha male was sinking balls-deep into her pussy.

"I will make this channel come even harder," Kil gritted out as he mounted her. His jaw clenched. "Who owns this flesh?" he asked arrogantly as one hand found her nipple ring, the other one found her navel ring, and he flicked rapidly at both.

Marty gasped as he sank into her to the hilt and rode her hard. His thrusts were deep and frenzied, and the look of unadulterated possessiveness on his face would have frightened her had she not known how much he loved her. *"You,"* she groaned, giving him the admission she knew he needed to hear. *"You own me."*

Kil rotated his hips and slammed home, oblivious to anyone or anything around him save his *nee'ka* and her lush channel. "By the Holy Law," he ground out as he pounded away into oblivion. "You are mine by the Holy Law."

He rung orgasm after orgasm out of her, sinking into her soaked flesh over and over, again and again. She needed that bridal necklace to pulse like she needed to breathe. She felt as though she was being driven to hysteria. He kept flicking at her Wani rings as he thrust into her, causing her to climax over and over again. *"Please,"* she begged in maddening desperation, *"give me your cum."*

"Mmmm," he purred, his hips rotating and grinding into hers, *"mine."* He closed his eyes and rode her harder and harder, mating her animalistically as he always did.

Marty reveled in his lust, for it never failed to amaze her how out of control Kil became while he was buried inside of her. When she had first joined the harem, she had seen how dispassionately he had screwed the other bound servants. But every time he sank into her body he moaned and groaned and thrust into her over and over again with an overwhelming euphoria that bordered on the maniacal.

"Kil." She wrapped her legs around his waist and moaned as her flesh enveloped his with lusty suctioning sounds. The sounds of their bodies and flesh slapping against each other, the feel of his tight balls slapping against her buttocks, the scent of their combined arousal...it was wicked. Delicious and wicked. *"Oh god."*

"Mari."

When he couldn't take anymore teasing, when he'd sank into her pussy until he'd found oblivion, only then did he grit his teeth and groan out his orgasm.

As the bridal necklace began to pulse, Marty's hands found his buttocks and squeezed. There were only three words that could describe how she felt just now, only three words that could convey the maddening euphoria of the moment.

"How. Fucking. Groovy."

Chapter Twenty-Six

℘

Cam's eyes narrowed suspiciously at the whispering he saw going on between Kara, Jana, and Dari. On this the moon-rising after the Consummation Feast when all should be paying homage to the bride, groom, and their girl child, the three princesses were sitting off by themselves across the great hall, whispering to one another under their breath rather than taking part in the celebratory, ritualistic function.

His eyes flicked to Gio. Gio also harbored an uneasy feeling about their hushed talk, he could tell. The warrior's eyes were narrowed and Cam could tell that his mood was grim. But then who could blame him? The embarrassment he had suffered from Dari's escapade at the shopping stalls was widely known and whispered about.

Gio's only solace had been in knowing that Dari's sire had publicly spanked her to teach her a lesson about betraying one's Sacred Mate. Or future Sacred Mate as it were. Still, Cam had spoken to the warrior and knew his anger was still at its apex, knew even that he desired to remove Dari from her birth home that her channel might be guarded by his own sire and *mani* until she was of an age where he could claim her. Cam wasn't certain whether or not Gio's request would be granted, but he knew for a certainty that the petition had been put before the emperor.

Cam's jaw clenched as his gaze darted back to Kara. She was excited about something and that made him uneasy. Kara was always apprehensive whenever he came to visit her at the palace, not giddy with excitement. And yet there she stood in all her dark beauty, whispering animatedly to her cousins.

Something was going on, he knew. Something he would not approve of.

And he would find out what that something was.

Chapter Twenty-Seven

ಬ

"My lord?"

Kara was careful to keep her eyes lowered as she slowly removed her *mazi* for Cam in the privacy of his suite that moon-rising. She hadn't wanted to come to him this eve for she didn't wish any guilt pangs to overtake her. The course had been set. The proverbial conveyance was in motion. There was no going back. "You wanted to speak with me?"

Cam said nothing, merely gazed at her nakedness as she disrobed for him. The lust in his glowing blue-green eyes aroused her as it always did and Kara felt her nipples plumping up for him. This, she told herself shakily, would simply not do.

Kara's gaze shot up warily to study his face. He had changed a lot over the years, growing from a laughing young warrior who had always teased her and made jests into an older warlord of thirty-nine Yessat years who rarely smiled and always managed to frighten her.

He was grim and she didn't have a care for it. But mayhap that's the price a warrior paid when the blood of so many was on his hands.

Kara was naïve and sheltered, but hardly stupid. Cam had started with nothing, had been born into this realm of lowly birth. He had fought for everything that was now his and would take no chances that any of it might be reclaimed. She admired him for his strength, yet paradoxically it was that very strength that frightened her so much.

From having been born to a lowly *trelli* sand miner, to becoming a hunter, to garnering his own sectors and ruling over them…such progressions did not take place without proving oneself by taking out the enemy in much battling.

She realized what she was to Cam K'al Ra. She didn't try to fool herself for a Nuba-minute. She was the ultimate trophy of battling prowess. There could be no greater marriage prize for a man born to a *trelli* miner that the daughter of the emperor, the daughter of the wealthiest and most powerful warlord of the time dimensions.

By virtue of their mother's lineage, Kara's sons would be proclaimed kings upon birth and her daughters would be princesses, even if not High Princesses as was she. Of course Cam K'al Ra coveted her, she thought sadly. Who could blame him? What warrior born to a *trelli* miner wouldn't? What warrior born to a king wouldn't for that matter?

But she wanted more from a Sacred Mate, she reminded herself. She wanted to be loved not as a battle prize, but as a woman. And thus was the reason that the course had been set.

"My lord?" she asked again, quieter this time. "You wished to see me?"

He said nothing as he slowly rose up from his chair, nothing as he strode over to her, nothing even as he picked her up and carried her to the raised bed.

"What are you doing?" Kara breathed out as he gently deposited her on the bed.

He slid her hips to the edge of it and nudged her thighs apart with his large hands. And still he said nothing.

"My lord?" she panted out as she came up on her elbows and glanced between her legs to see what he was about.

Cam's gaze clashed with hers as his thumb found her clit and worked it around in methodic circles. Kara gasped as she stared down at him.

"There is no escape from me," he murmured. "Not now. Not ever."

Her eyes darted about warily. He was suspicious and that wouldn't do for a certainty. "I-I don't know what you mean," she said with feigned surprise.

"Aye you do." His tongue shot out and he licked one long path from the opening of her channel to her clit. Only then did he raise his head. "Heed my words well, Kara. Do not force me to punish you."

Cam summoned her gaze and held it for a protracted moment, showing her but the smallest display of the dominance nature had given his body over hers. He could command her to his will by wishing it done, make it so her body was immobile and thereby unable to flee if he so chose.

Kara's eyes widened. She had never felt so penetrated, so commanded to another's will. And this by his gaze alone.

By the goddess, she thought as he broke the mysterious hold on her and buried his face between her thighs to lap her into orgasm, this would not do for a certainty.

* * * * *

"Papa?" Dari asked softly. Her glowing blue gaze shot towards her mother. "*Mani*? What is wrong?"

Geris swiped at her tears and ran from the apartments they kept in Sand City, too emotional to speak.

Dari felt an icy chill of foreboding creep down her spine. That wasn't like her mother for a certainty. Her mother never fled from a chamber in upset. She always stayed and held her own, no matter her state of mind. "Papa?" she asked quietly, noting for the first time that his eyes looked bloodshot from crying. "Papa what has happened?"

"My brother..." he began hoarsely, his voice trailing off.

"Aye?"

Dak took a deep breath. "The emperor has granted Gio's petition," he muttered, turning around to pace the chamber.

175

Dari's eyes rounded. Her hearts' rate sped up. "What petition?" she choked out.

Dak stopped his pacing and swung around to face her. He ran a punishing hand through his golden hair. "A fortnight from now, when Gio returns to his homeland for good, you will accompany him. And," he rasped out, "'tis where you will remain."

"Nay," she gasped, her stomach churning. She felt as though she was going to be sick. "Nay, papa, please do not make me." She ran towards him and threw her arms around his middle. "Please," she cried, "'tis sorry I am to have shamed you. Please do not make me go!"

Dak plucked her up from the ground and held her tight. "I was given no choice, *ty'ka*," he said hoarsely. "Your uncle thinks it prudent to strike this bargain that our two houses do not come to blows." He sighed. "The King of Arak feels that you have shamed his son and desires that you be handed over immediately in an effort to save face."

"Nay," Dari whispered against her sire's neck. Tears tracked down her cheeks. "Nay."

"You will be treated with every care," Dak said gently, trying to rein in his upset and anger on his daughter's behalf that she might not be frightened for the future. He stroked her back. "I have not a care for the King of Arak, yet 'tis for a certainty he will take no chances with your welfare." He went on to explain, "Your betrothed is his only heir. He knows that his future dwells within your womb."

Dari couldn't speak. She was numb—numb with shock and grief.

"Gio's training in the warring arts is complete. He will return to Arak to build his own forces. He will care for you well, *pani*."

Dari sobbed in her sire's arms for long minutes and Dak made no move to stop her. He let her have her cry because for a certainty she deserved it. When at last she raised her head and her glowing blue eyes so much like his own found his, she had but one question. "Will I ever see you and *mani* again?" she whispered.

"Aye." Dak gently nudged her face against his chest again. His jaw clenched. "When Gio permits you to visit us."

* * * * *

"I can't believe you!"

Zor grimaced as he ducked to miss yet another flying bottle of vintage *mutpow*. In all of the Yessat years he had spent at her side, Kyra had never been so angered with him.

"'Twas the honorable decision!" he bellowed, plucking his *nee'ka* up off of the ground to keep her from hurdling more bottles at him. "Dari committed a wrong, Gio was angered, as the representative of the Arak dynasty his sire demanded they be permitted to save face." He placed her on the raised bed, then threw his hands into the air. "What was I to do? Had she been any other girl-child but my niece I wouldn't have hesitated in granting the request!"

"My own best friend," Kyra said through narrowed eyes as she shook a finger at him. "Because of you my own best friend will not speak to me!"

"She will calm down."

"Ha!"

Zor ran a hand through his hair and grunted. "My brother is not speaking to me either, if it makes you feel better to know this."

"No!" she wailed. "It doesn't!"

"Kyra," he sighed, "you are giving me the headache for a certainty."

"Good!"

"Kyra," he growled warningly.

She took a deep breath. "I don't know, Zor, maybe you did what is considered the right thing in Trek Mi Q'an." She

177

shook her head. "But the fact that the warriors of Trek Mi Q'an consider removing a fourteen-year-old child from her home the honorable thing to do—and for doing nothing more than shyly telling a warrior he was handsome no less!—brings home everything that is wrong with this place." Her nostrils flared. "She is a scared little girl, not a face-saving trophy. You have treated her like a sacrificial lamb and I don't know that I can ever forgive you for that."

"Kyra," Zor murmured, "please do not say that."

She experienced a pang of guilt, since she was able to feel his emotions and knew that he was hurting. But a bigger issue was at stake. A bigger issue than her husband's feelings, a bigger issue even than Dari being carted off to Arak.

"Something terrible is going to come of this," she whispered. "Something that will affect us all." She stared into space unblinking. "Ari has foretold it."

Zor's entire body stilled. "What has she foretold?" he asked warily.

Kyra went into his arms willingly, needing his comfort. "She isn't certain," she said quietly. "She only knows that a danger to all of us is coming."

"Because of the bargain I struck?" he said in a rasp.

"No." She hugged him tighter. "But that was the catalyst."

Chapter Twenty-Eight

෨

"I'm so glad she appeared to me while I was dying, so you know she's still watching out for you." Marty sighed. "Oh Kil I'm so sorry."

She ran her hand over his strong jaw line after he finished telling her about the day he had lost his mother on Tron. She closed her eyes briefly and took a deep breath. "Your courage amazes me. I don't think I could ever be so strong."

Kil looked at her as though she had gone daft. "Surely you jest, Mari. Never have I met a stronger or more resilient humanoid than you."

He smiled as he looked at her, never having thought it was possible to be this vastly content. Alone in the apartments he kept at the Palace of the Dunes, the deuce of them in ignorance of the mayhem brewing below stairs, his *nee'ka* was snuggling against him in his lap whilst she breastfed wee Zy'an.

Marty grinned. "I must say, Mighty One, that your wench wooing is progressing in leaps and bounds. You'll have to add an addendum to that handbook of yours. Compliments will get you everywhere, you know."

He grunted. "Mayhap I should add a chapter that deals specifically with taming *heeka-beasts*. 'Tis a fine art not easily cultivated."

She chuckled as she gently lifted Zy'an from her breasts and handed her daughter over to the wench wooer for burping. "I doubt the warriors who read the handbook will head off to Koror on a bride-quest."

Kil lifted Zy'an onto his shoulder and gently patted her back. "I would have," he said softly as his gaze found Marty's.

"I would have faced off every predator on Tryston and beyond to bring you back to me."

Her heart melted as it always did when King Grim & Gruff said such sweet things to her. Especially since she knew that he meant them. She could feel his hearts beating rapidly, knew that he was wanting to hold her as close as a man could hold a woman because his need to be with her was always so all-consuming.

"Tell me you love me," Kil murmured.

Marty smiled. He needed the love words. She could say them a thousand times a day and he'd still ask her in that arrogant way of his to say them again.

She stretched up and kissed his lips. "I love you, Kil. I love you with all of my heart."

He grinned. "And I love you with all of my two hearts."

"Pig," she teased.

"*Heeka-beast*," he teased back.

They chuckled as their lips came together in a kiss.

Epilogue
Jioti Sector of Planet Tryston
One week later

☙

He, a warrior not given to jest, had made sport of Kil for being too much the dunce to recognize his own Sacred Mate upon seeing her.

A tic began to work in Death's jaw as he strode from the conveyance launching pad and toward his estate. He was as much the bedamned dunce as was his friend.

He had figured out that Kari belonged to him whilst attending the Consummation Feast. Try as he might, when the feast had finished he hadn't been able to summon enough desire to take any of the bound servants back to the *vesha* hides. There had been but one channel he had desired to sample of, only one woman whose visage had lingered in his mind.

But she was gone.

He had instructed Kari to await his return in Crystal City before he had left for the feast. She had not waited. According to her former employer, she had hightailed it out of the sector the moment Death had turned his back. 'Twas sore apparent that the Galian wench thought to deny him his rights by eluding him.

Death grunted as he strode into his great hall and summoned himself a goblet of moonshine *matpow*. Were he not so bedamned angry at her for deliberately disobeying him he would have laughed. She could run, aye, but she was naught but daft if she truly believed he would not hunt her down. She belonged to him. He could do naught else.

181

Seating himself at the raised table, he laid his head back on the breasts of the bound servant massaging his shoulders. There had been a time when she had been his favored. Now he would give her to Gio as a gift.

Gio. The fully trained High Lord had not been himself since having learned of Princess Dari's behavior at the trading stalls on Ti Q'won. Truly, Death now wished he had said nothing to him. The young beauty had done naught but shyly flirt, yet Gio had taken the news as though the princess had invited him to sample of her virgin channel.

Death's eyes narrowed as he asked himself what he would do if he learned that Kari had so much as flirted with another warrior after fleeing from him. He grunted. He would kill the warrior is what he would do.

Death sighed. He supposed Gio's grim mood was understandable after all.

Picking up his goblet, his thoughts turned to Kari as he sipped from it. He would find her the soonest, he silently vowed, and when he did he would never let her go again. He had come back to Jioti to regroup for a spell, to gather his hunters that they might aid him on his bride-quest.

He needed Kari's sweet, luscious channel. He needed her greedy, voracious mouth. And, he admitted with a resolved sigh, he needed *her*—period.

He was a fool for having not recognized her in the first, he knew—a fool who would never again rest easy until she was firmly back under his dominion.

Love of the hearts. When he had been captured all of those years back, he had been told 'twould never be his. The evil one had made him believe those words, had made him believe he was a dead man walking.

Death. It had named him Death. And he had offered the evil one no resistance for he had believed it.

But Kari was his. He knew she was. And that meant that the evil one had lied. Mayhap if it had lied about that, it had lied about other things as well. There was but one way to find out.

But before he could do aught else, before he could allow himself to find the answers, he needed to hunt down the key to his redemption, the woman whose very existence gave his purpose. He needed Kari. And when he found her, he would never let her go.

* * * * *

"We were told your people might be willing to help us."

Kara gulped a bit nervously as she, Jana, and Dari spoke to the Galian woman on the receiving end of the holo-communication. "We need help the soonest, before the bridal necklaces are clasped about our necks and—"

"Bridal necklaces?" the Galian woman murmured. "Are you speaking of those necklaces warriors wear with colorful gems threaded through them?"

Kara glanced toward Jana. She found the question a bit odd, having incorrectly assumed that all peoples of Trek Mi Q'an understood the ways of Trystonni mating. "Aye."

"What do these necklaces do?" the Galian inquired softly.

Dari's nostrils flared. "They chain you for life to a warrior uncaring of your feelings, to a warrior who sees you as naught more than a receptacle of his lust and a breeder of his heirs." Her eyes narrowed. "She who is clasped will know naught but grief, sadness, and a lifetime of having her every dream and desire denied her. She will be given no independence, granted no choices, for verily she is reduced to the status of possession."

Kara's eyebrows rose. A bit dramatic, mayhap, yet effective.

"So will you aid us?" Jana asked. "We can pay you for your trouble, for we've bartered *qi'kas* for credits."

The Galian glanced at her sisters before turning back to the princesses. "You are royal, are you not?"

Kara nibbled on her bottom lip. "How did you know that?"

The Galian smiled. "I used to share the same name as you, but when I came to Trek Mi Q'an I had to change it because it's forbidden by the Holy Law for a non-royal man or woman to share the name of a member of the emperor's direct line. If your name is Kara, it's not a giant leap in logic to figure out just whose daughter you are."

Kara sighed. "He will hunt for me, my sire will. I cannot lie to you when you think to show me a kindness. If you are to aid us, we want you to know the truth in full that you might understand the forces we would all be up against."

The Galian inclined her head. "Your honesty is appreciated." She smiled, showing off two dimples that further reminded Kara of her *mani*. The resemblance between the two women was nigh unto spooky. "But to be honest," the Galian continued, "my sisters and I welcome the challenge."

"So you'll aid us?" Jana asked excitedly.

The Galian nodded her head. "We will. However long it takes you to escape your respective prisons, feel secure in the knowledge that Galis will be your salvation."

Dari's eyes lit up. "Even if it takes us a year or mayhap two to escape, you will truly not forget us?"

"No. A promise made by a Galian woman is a promise kept." She grimaced, thinking about a certain promise she'd made and then deliberately broken to a warrior she couldn't stop thinking about. But that had been different, she reminded herself, vastly different.

Kara smiled. "Thank-you ever so much, kind mistress. Might I inquire as to the name you now go by?"

The Galian smiled. "Kari," she said. "Kari Gy'at Li."

* * * * *

Dari swiped at the tears that tracked down her cheeks as she turned around to wave goodbye to her *mani* and papa. Her sisters stood upon the conveyance launching pad of the Palace of the Dunes huddled together and crying. Even Dar, the bedamned brother she loved regardless to everything, looked as though he might shed a tear for her leave taking.

But she didn't want them to be sad, not even Dar, so she raised her hand and attempted a forced smile as she waved to them. They waved back, however half-heartedly, and she took a deep breath to steady herself.

Dari's gaze flicked towards her sire. He was crying softly, trying to pretend that he wasn't. But she knew him too well, could read his emotions almost as well as her *mani* could. He felt grief for her leave taking, not to mention powerfully guilty for spanking her, and she didn't want him to feel that way at all. She didn't blame her sire, and truth be told she wasn't even angry at him anymore.

Nay. If there was one to blame it was the warrior holding onto her elbow just now trying to prod her along.

Tearing her elbow away from Gio Z'an Tar, Dari flew towards her father and into his arms. "Do not grieve for me," she whispered, choking back her own tears. "I love you, papa, and I shall prevail."

Dak closed his eyes and held her tightly, smelling her scent as he had so many times when she'd been a tiny hatchling. "For a certainty you will come home soon to visit, *ty'ka*. 'Tis a vow."

Dari didn't know if that were true, for the course had been set and the appointed day would be soon. But she hugged him back tightly and smiled against his chest. "Take care of *mani*, aye? Do not let her keep a temper with Auntie."

Dak smiled. "Aye," he said roughly. He set her down on the ground, his eyes locking with his future son-within-the-law's who awaited Dari patiently a few feet away. "Go on." He gently nudged his daughter towards her betrothed. "'Twill all work out, *pani*. Gio will care for you well."

She doubted her father's logic, but said nothing more on the subject. She kissed his cheek instead, then offered the same to her quietly crying mother and siblings.

"Let us go," Gio said gently as he took Dari by the arm.

She obediently left with him, her head held proudly as she walked towards his high-speed conveyance, but she would not look at him, which pained him more than he cared to admit.

No matter. She belonged to him now and would never be far from his sight again. And, he reminded himself, when at long last they were joined she would never desire to leave him again for 'twould hurt her just as much as him in the doing.

Nevertheless, Gio Z'an Tar was no fool. As he lifted the princess into his conveyance and took the seat next to hers, he conceded that the next eleven Yessat years might be very difficult indeed. Dari was determined not to like him, determined even to hate him, and penetrating her icy façade would be no easy feat.

But he could do it. Given time and patience he knew that he could.

* * * * *

Dari's glowing blue eyes found Jana's as the conveyance prepared for take-off. Her elder sister's gaze was fiercely determined and Dari blew out a breath of relief at seeing it. Jana might carry the look of their sire, but 'twas their *mani's* unrelenting personality that made up who she was.

Aye, her sister would show on the prearranged day for a certainty. 'Twas naught to fear on that score. Dari settled back into her seat and closed her eyes, pacified in the knowledge that all would be well.

From beside her Gio said nothing, though he had seen the odd look that the sisters had shared between them. They were up to something for a certainty.

Gio glanced down suspiciously at his sleeping betrothed. He would have to keep an extra close vigil on Dari until he knew what that something was.

Why an electronic book?

We live in the Information Age—an exciting time in the history of human civilization, in which technology rules supreme and continues to progress in leaps and bounds every minute of every day. For a multitude of reasons, more and more avid literary fans are opting to purchase e-books instead of paper books. The question from those not yet initiated into the world of electronic reading is simply: *Why?*

1. *Price.* An electronic title at Ellora's Cave Publishing and Cerridwen Press runs anywhere from 40% to 75% less than the cover price of the exact same title in paperback format. Why? Basic mathematics and cost. It is less expensive to publish an e-book (no paper and printing, no warehousing and shipping) than it is to publish a paperback, so the savings are passed along to the consumer.

2. *Space.* Running out of room in your house for your books? That is one worry you will never have with electronic books. For a low one-time cost, you can purchase a handheld device specifically designed for e-reading. Many e-readers have large, convenient screens for viewing. Better yet, hundreds of titles can be stored within your new library—on a single microchip. There are a variety of e-readers from different manufacturers. You can also read e-books on your PC or laptop computer. (Please note that Ellora's Cave does not endorse any specific brands.

You can check our websites at www.ellorascave.com or www.cerridwenpress.com for information we make available to new consumers.)

3. *Mobility.* Because your new e-library consists of only a microchip within a small, easily transportable e-reader, your entire cache of books can be taken with you wherever you go.

4. *Personal Viewing Preferences.* Are the words you are currently reading too small? Too large? Too... ANNOYING? Paperback books cannot be modified according to personal preferences, but e-books can.

5. *Instant Gratification.* Is it the middle of the night and all the bookstores near you are closed? Are you tired of waiting days, sometimes weeks, for bookstores to ship the novels you bought? Ellora's Cave Publishing sells instantaneous downloads twenty-four hours a day, seven days a week, every day of the year. Our webstore is never closed. Our e-book delivery system is 100% automated, meaning your order is filled as soon as you pay for it.

Those are a few of the top reasons why electronic books are replacing paperbacks for many avid readers.

As always, Ellora's Cave and Cerridwen Press welcome your questions and comments. We invite you to email us at Comments@ellorascave.com or write to us directly at Ellora's Cave Publishing Inc., 1056 Home Avenue, Akron, OH 44310-3502.

erridwen, the Celtic Goddess of wisdom, was the muse who brought inspiration to storytellers and those in the creative arts. Cerridwen Press encompasses the best and most innovative stories in all genres of today's fiction. Visit our site and discover the newest titles by talented authors who still get inspired - much like the ancient storytellers did, once upon a time.

Cerridwen Press

www.cerridwenpress.com

Discover for yourself why readers can't get enough of the multiple award-winning publisher

Ellora's Cave.

Whether you prefer e-books or paperbacks,

be sure to visit EC on the web at
www.ellorascave.com

for an erotic reading experience that will leave you breathless.